UNEARTHLY

Corinne's story
continues in...

STARCROSSED

and

ASCENDED

[coming soon]

ALSO BY KATIE JANE GALLAGHER

The Gold in the Dark
(free at katiejgallagher.com)

Specter

Beauty and Her Alien series

Unearthly
Starcrossed

HIDDEN
BOWER

ISBN: 978-1-7377895-0-5

First Edition First Printing
Cover Illustration Copyright © 2021 by LianaM.
Old Retro Labels TFB font by zanatlija.
Sexything font by Xavier Puig.
Optimus Princeps font by Manfred Klein.

www.katiejgallagher.com

UNEARTHLY

KATIE JANE GALLAGHER

HIDDEN
BOWER

One

Beauty despaired at the thought that this castle was to be her eternal prison and her only companion its beastly master.

And the Beast, no dumb creature, despaired as well. For if this houseguest, so lovely, kind, and brave, could not see past his unhuman shell to the soul within, then what use he to live?

Chapter One

THE MOMENT JOE WALKED INTO THE SHOP THAT NIGHT I KNEW I'd let things go on far too long.

I'm an early bird by all definitions, but I've been on the late shift ever since Kris had her baby last spring. Not that she's left the shop for good—she's on the call list if one of the college kids doesn't show—but babies keep their own timetable, and an eight-o'clock close, which means you're actually walking out the door eight forty-five-ish, just wasn't going to cut it anymore. And I'm the most reliable of all our bunch, and the one who's been there the longest besides, so when my boss, Ray, sat me down and asked nicely if I'd consider coming in a bit later, and oh, by the way, how about a two-dollar-per-hour raise—well, I said okay. Two dollars more an hour is almost enough to make working at a kayak-and-ski shop respectable when you're twenty-three years old.

Not that the shop is unrespectable. People like us, and we get great online ratings—a full star more than Ski and Sail in Scarlettville, the next town over. That's all down to Ray, who makes sure to run a tight ship (har har) since we get all sorts—racers, people looking to rent, middle-aged guys with money to burn, paddleboard pussies (Evan's term, not mine). Our ski inventory is top notch, and we have kayaks that run the gamut from entry-level to whatever model Sail Freak has listed as the latest and greatest. Plus all the accessories you could ever want and refurbishing services, too. And the Big Deer River is right out back, or the Big D to anyone with even the mildest sense of humor, which makes it easy for us to run lessons for kids and beginners. So I can understand how you could hear the words *kayak-and-ski shop* and think it's a basic operation, and keeping the shop alive and gasping *is* pretty much second nature to me after six years—but what I'm trying to say is that there's more to it than you'd think, and me doing Ray a favor and taking the late shift for a little while, which soon turned into a longer while, was one of those things that count for more than what they seem.

But the shift didn't agree with me. I like going into work, doing my time, then having the rest of the day to myself. Flipping that schedule on its head made me tired and lazy; I'd never been so permanently behind on laundry, nor so familiar with Bamboo Garden's takeout menu. There was also the added complication that I don't like driving on Fett's Gap Mountain Road at night, which is the route you have to take to get from the shop back to my house. I mean, I'll do it if I have to, but I'll do pretty much anything *not* to.

I'd actually worked matters out so that the driving thing wasn't a big issue. My best friend Molly and I close together on

Mondays and Wednesdays, and she didn't mind me carpooling back with her. But save for Sundays, which is my consistent day off and a prize hard fought for and carefully guarded, all the other days it's Evan and I who close up, and that was becoming a problem. *Not* with Evan—out of all the college kids on our crew, he's the best by far. Shows up on time, doesn't think he's above retail, doesn't exhale sarcasm like the other college kids, good conversationalist. Just a real sweetheart (save for his severe prejudice against paddleboarders). And he was totally fine with driving me home whenever we closed together—but Joe had increasingly been giving indications that he was not fine with that.

Joe and I had been *a thing* for a bit—a nebulous, amoebic thing that I had a hard time looking at straight. We'd managed to hit all the initial benchmarks of two people who are moving towards establishing a relationship: a tipsy make-out session at a late-summer pool party to kick things off, then a proper movie date. Then some more dates: hiking, milkshakes and chili dogs at Arlene's Bar and Grill, a requisite kayaking trip down the Big D. When we talked, the conversation was good. He was courteous, handsome, owned his own landscaping business. We hadn't slept together yet, but surely he'd be great. On paper, he was perfect. But everything we were together, and everything we'd done, somehow felt like a bunch of puzzle pieces that didn't quite match up.

That, and there was something about his face sometimes when I looked at him sidelong, when he didn't know I was watching. A part of him that he kept tucked out of sight, only rising to the surface in odd, fleeting moments. I couldn't say I felt like I *knew* him.

It was a hard thing to put into words, so I tried to talk around it to Molly, circling a murky bull's-eye that I didn't understand. "The issue," I said to her one day as we were leaving the shop, "is that everyone likes those things. Kissing, milkshakes, and kayaking."

The headlights of her old Civic winked at us as she unlocked it. "Not everyone likes kayaking."

"The good ones do."

She snorted. "Like you have so much experience. You barely dated before Joe."

"We're not *dating*," I said, shutting the car door more firmly than necessary.

Her blue eyes bored into me. Molly might be short, but she's intimidating when she needs to be. "And what else would you call it?"

"Individual dates. That just happen to be with the same person."

"And what does one plus one equal?"

"He's just so…" I tugged on my braid as I grasped for words. I like to keep my hair out of my face while I'm working; anything else is just asking for trouble. All the long-haired girls can probably relate: it's oh-so-fun to have a mane, but at the same time I am forever getting it caught in things or dragging it through my food accidentally. Also, having it down is a magnet for customer flirtation—guys like blondes with big boobs, go figure—which was exhilarating when I first started working at the shop, but now is just an annoyance. "…so urgh," I finished lamely.

Molly started the car. "Then give me urgh any day. Joe's hot."

"Yes, technically. I just don't know if—"

"And he's a good kisser," she said, pulling out of the parking lot. "You said that."

I fidgeted in the seat as my eyes bounced from one side of the road to the other, on the lookout for deer. Mating season runs through early December, so we still had a week or so left before their numbers would drop off. "Again, yes. Technically." Joe knew his way around a woman's mouth, but wasn't being with the right guy supposed to be a bit more melty? Books were always talking about pulse-racing kisses, knee-buckling kisses, kisses to make your cheeks hot and nether regions pulse with lust. Against that admittedly unscientific benchmark, Joe was… maybe a five?

But it could be my standards were too high. Molly certainly thought so.

"Corinne, listen to me." Her voice sank into her *I'm-going-to-Mom-at-you-right-now* register. "He has a car and a good, stable job and his own place. And he's not an EMT." This was always a plus in Molly's book, who had *stories* from the EMT she'd dated briefly before getting back together with her now-husband. "Or a heroin addict!" Yet more stories. "Choose Joe. *Choose Joe.*"

"Yeah," I said, watching the headlights split the night in two, Moses-like. There weren't streetlights this far out of town. "I don't know. I mean, he's bought IMAX tickets for *Out of the Aether* this Saturday. So I'll see how that goes." I tried to inject some conviction into my voice, as if a night spent watching guys blow things up with ray guns was going to help me decide the future of… whatever this was.

But I was spared the movie, because on Friday, with just a few minutes till close, Joe strolled through the door.

Evan and I were deep into a discussion about aliens as we straightened up the shelves, sparked by the release of *Out of the Aether*, which he was going to see that night at its midnight release. Evan's a firm believer, especially when he's just taken a couple hits from his vape pen out back. Me, I'd always been more of a skeptic, but I saw no harm in letting Evan have his fun, just like I always let my Aunt Misty go on about the ghost in her house and her latest favorite angel.

"Just think about the numbers," Evan was saying. "The amount of stars in the universe. The amount of planets."

"Mm-hm."

"I read an article the other day that said there are about twenty billion trillion stars."

"Wow, twenty *batrillion*?"

He shot me a withering, red-eyed look. "Shut up, Corinne. So, you take all those stars, some of them are going to have planets just the right amount away that you're not freezing off or burning away all potential life. Conservatively, that gets us down to, say, five billion trillion stars. Then you whittle away all the stars with orbiting planets that are the right distance away but still have issues—no water, the wrong gases, stuff like that—and maybe we only have a couple billion trillion so-called perfect solar systems now to choose from. How many of them have allowed life to form? What about intelligent life? Civilization? Technology?"

My eyes drifted to the clock—five minutes till close. "Sounds about as likely as winning the lottery."

He shook his head. "But when you crunch the numbers we're still talking about literally billions of solar systems. And all it takes is one to—"

But the creak of the door cut short his building soliloquy. A red bolt of anger shot through me; what customer dared cross the threshold of Wakpa Paddling and Ski Center at this hour? Then I turned around, my shopgirl smile pasted on and my *we're-just-about-to-close* voice ready to deploy, and my anger cooled to annoyance when I saw Joe striding towards me.

And with that annoyance came a cool, hard certainty that this was over. No matter how great this man might be on paper, no matter how strong his jaw or model-like his dark hair, no matter how much Molly loved living vicariously through my dating life, something about him chafed at me like fine-grit sandpaper.

"Hey," I said to him as my thoughts raced. How and when was I going to do this? Surely it was best to get the breakup over with as soon as possible.

"Hey, babe." His blue eyes darted over to Evan, and he raised his chin. "'Sup?" Then his gaze was back on me, and he treated me to a beaming smile, his perfectly aligned teeth the brightest thing in the shop. A movie-star smile. Molly was going to flay me alive for breaking up with this man.

I drew a breath. "So... what are you doing here?"

"Just thought I'd drop by and give you a ride once you're done. You feel like stopping for burgers? My treat."

"Umm…"

"Ooh," Evan cut in, stoner eyes bright. "Where you going to go? Arlene's? The Roadhouse?"

"Lady's choice, of course," Joe said with another smile at me.

"I don't know that I'm up for burgers," I said. "My stomach's been feeling a bit off."

Evan raised his eyebrows. "But we just had those cupcakes, what, like an hour ago? Joe, you want a cupcake? Ray's wife brought them in…"

Damn it, Evan, shut up. "I think it might have been the cupcake that did it," I said, then offered a silent apology to Ray's wife, whose wonderful cupcakes didn't deserve the lie.

"I'll take you home," Joe said smoothly. He turned back to Evan. "Listen, since she feels sick, you can close up yourself, right?"

If Evan were a puppy, Joe would be Cesar Millan. Evan's eyes widened slightly, then he gave a sharp nod. There's some magnetic quality about Joe that makes other people, especially other guys, straighten up and listen. Hence him owning Wakpa's most successful landscaping company at twenty-seven.

I, meanwhile, was swiftly slipping from annoyance back to anger. "But he's just an associate—sorry, Evan, but it's true. I still have to close out, write the log—"

Evan was fighting back a smile. "Here's the log: 'It's Friday night. Nobody comes in Friday nights because they're all at Arlene's. We haven't had a customer in since five, so why the hell do we have to be here until eight?' Relax, Corinne, I got this. You go home and rest up."

"But—"

"*Go.*" And I saw that his shoulders were set, my battle lost. Feeling more than a little like a person in the process of being kidnapped, I grabbed my things, then trailed Joe out the front door to his gleaming truck—a new purchase, which still reeked of new-car smell. As it started up, I cast a desperate look back at the warm, familiar comfort of the shop. Evan gave me a cheery wave through the window as we backed up, then we jetted off into the night.

Chapter Two

"WHAT WAS THAT BACK THERE?" I ASKED HIM AS WE PLOWED through the darkness. My nails dug half-circles into my palms. Joe liked getting his money's worth out of the new engine.

He turned to look at me, a smile playing on his lips. "What do you mean?"

"You dropping by the shop. Getting Evan to close up."

He raised an eyebrow. "Burgers, babe. Thought I'd surprise you. And he's not a kid; he can handle it." He was silent for a moment, the hum of the engine the only sound. Then: "But you know, you're smart. It wasn't just about burgers."

I'd thought as much. "Yeah?"

"Yeah," he said, taking a curve in the road faster than necessary. My hands went white-knuckled. "I mean, first of all, you're not feeling good, so of course he should close up for you. That's just common decency. And second of all, he's a stoner. I mean, he was obviously high back there."

"He's always good to go by the time we're leaving." This was true, plus Evan always made sure to take the drive real slow for me.

"Still, better for you not to ride with someone like that. And his car's kind of a shitbox."

I took almost personal offense to that. "But I *like* his shitbox. Agatha's got character." Evan drove an old police cruiser he'd bought at auction. She'd seen some things, and she creaked ominously whenever he took downhill left turns, but he drove her with reverence, like the stately dowager she was.

"It's unsafe. And…" He grimaced. "Well, I hate to say this, but I think he's into you."

I inhaled sharply as the car sped over the beginnings of a pothole. It would be a crater by February. "Would you mind slowing down a bit?" It was the witching hour for deer.

A muscle twitched at the side of Joe's mouth; was this funny to him? My irritation swelled.

"Anyway," I continued, "he's definitely not. Into me, I mean." I knew this for a fact; Evan always got all starry-eyed when he worked with Gabriella, our newest college kid. He'd never once looked that way at me.

But Joe's expression said he wasn't convinced. "Come on, of course he's into you. Anyone would be. You're gorgeous. Kind. Caring."

"Thanks." *Thanks, and I'm sorry about this, but let's break up.* "So, what, you just thought you'd pick me up from now on whenever Evan and I close together?"

He brightened. "Not the most terrible idea, right? And…" He let out a breath as his hand slid from the steering wheel to my knee. "Well, I've been thinking about some other things, too."

I had a sudden, crawling instinct that our conversation had

veered into uncharted waters, very possibly rife with sharks.

"This is just so *right* between us." Joe barked a little laugh, shaking his head, and his hand tightened on my knee. "You know, I've dated other girls but I've never felt... Well, I guess I'll just say it. I love you. Can't hardly believe it, but there it is."

Oh God. Oh no. And now he'd want me to say it back...

But no, he was continuing on, with the cadence of someone reciting a long, concocted speech. "And I'm sure you've guessed I feel that way about you by now. I know it's soon, I know it's crazy—but we should move in together. There, I've said it. Corinne? Hey, Corinne, what's wrong?"

I did my best to keep my voice steady, even as my cheeks heated up. "I don't... feel that way towards you. And I don't think that would be a good idea."

The speed of the car faltered—hallelujah. "I know it's early, babe. I get that. There's no rush to say it back. But moving in together would be good for us. You'll see. Once we—"

"No, Joe. You're great, but I've been thinking we should... see other people?" Every syllable from my lips was a Herculean effort. The air in the car had gone all hot and syrupy, the heater up a tad too high.

"But—"

"No. I'm sorry, but I'm not going to move in with you." I couldn't look at him, opting instead to stare out the window into the dark. If we did hit a deer and die, at least that would put an end to this conversation.

A few torturous seconds ticked by. "Because of your dad," he said slowly. "He likes you living at home. He wouldn't approve."

Well, that might be true, but it was beside the point. "That's not it. He likes you. I know he might have given you the tough dad talk when you came by the house, but—"

"Then what is it, Corinne? Because *this*"—he thrust a hand at the empty air between us—"is a good thing, and I'm having a hard time understanding how you can't see that."

What do you say when any answer you could give is just fuzzy instinct? I was trying to string words together when his next sentence bowled me over the head. "You're cheating on me, aren't you?" His voice had gone flat. "With Evan."

I goggled at him, flabbergasted. "I am actually *not* cheating on you. How can you say that?"

He huffed out a breath. "I saw you two through the window when I drove up. Saw how you were joking around with him."

My jaw was about on the floor. "And you think I'm seeing any guy I joke around with?" I shook my head wonderingly. What reality was he living in? Had he never been turned down before by a woman?

I shivered as he shot me another look: eyes hard and flinty, mouth set in a thin line. That was the moment I became acutely aware that I was being driven in a car by a man who was very, very upset with me. A man who, perhaps, was not often told no.

"Again," I said slowly, "I am not cheating on you." And I let my right hand fall off my lap and slip inside my purse, feeling for my phone. Not that he'd do anything, surely; Joe's the type of guy where people always have some nice story to tell about him. Loved by all—well, everyone except me, I guess, and that was what really counted right now in this slow-moving train wreck of an evening.

So I fumbled for my phone and said, "Let's just get back to the house and we can talk about this. Maybe I'm shy of commitment. So we can talk about it. About moving in together."

"Yeah?" His eyes held mine, and I winced.

"Yeah, but can you please just watch the ro—oh!" For a dark streak of fur had just bounded out of the forest straight towards the car.

We missed the first one; they say that's how it always goes. The second deer, though, we hit square on. A thunk and the sound of splintering glass. The squeal of brakes as we careened left. Lurching toward the windshield, before the seatbelt bit into my shoulder and wrenched me back. The car had stopped, I could feel that, but my heart was beating at a sprinter's pace.

It had finally happened, the thing I'd feared so long realized again. The thing that never left me, stuck to my subconscious like a stubborn burr.

"Corinne?" I opened my eyes to Joe's white face. "Are you all right?" His voice was oddly distant.

"F-fine." The world spun around me.

"You didn't hit your head or anything?" He scanned me for injury, his hand brushing my arm.

"Don't touch me!"

He drew back sharply, like a snake recoiling, then regarded me for a long, strange moment before casting a look around. "All right. We're blocking the other lane." He reached back over to the steering wheel. "I'm just going to pull ov—"

But I was scrabbling with the seatbelt, not ready to be driven another inch by this man. With a click the belt released its death grip, and I opened the door. "No, I'm getting out of this *fucking* car."

His brow knit into a frown, but before he could say anything I half-stepped half-fell out into the winter night. The pavement was wobbly under my feet, like I was a sailor stepping back onto dry land after months at sea. Utter silence from behind me; the truck didn't move, and I could feel him watching me.

I called my dad as I made my way over to the shoulder. I expected to see the deer slumped on the road, but the asphalt was empty, save for black skid marks from the tires. The truck was real banged up on the right side—the headlight shattered, a chunk of the bumper hanging off to scrape the pavement—but the deer had at least been of sound-enough health to leave the scene. I was panting, each breath a little stabbing knife of cold.

My dad answered just as his voicemail was about to kick in. "What's up, sweetheart?"

"W-we got in an accident over on Fett's Gap. Joe and I. Hit a deer. Can you come?" It would be nice if my voice stopped quavering.

"You're all right?" His cheery tone had gone all low and serious. "You call an ambulance?"

"I'm fine. Can you just come?"

"On my way," he said and hung up.

By this point Joe had pulled the truck over and was out of the car surveying the damage, accompanied by a few muttered curses. The hazard lights were a blinking spotlight that did little to press back the darkness of the woods on either side of the road. In my peripheral vision, I saw Joe turn his head toward me like he was thinking of saying something, but then he ran a hand through his hair and bent again to look at the truck. Dimly, I wondered what the deer was doing right now—if it would escape this night with just a nasty bruise or if it was in the process of dying.

There came a glow of headlights from behind us. Not my dad—it would be a few more minutes yet before he got here. The approaching driver gave a quick double honk and pulled over.

"Hey there!" said an older male voice as the driver's side door opened. "Joe Gagnon, that you? Run into some car trouble?" Like I said, Joe's pretty well-liked around town, and it wasn't surprising that whoever this was knew him in some way or another.

"Yeah," Joe called. "Hi, Ted."

It took a moment of squinting around the headlights before I realized I recognized the speaker: a portly man with a white beard in a down coat and jeans that I'd seen working at Arlene's Bar and Grill. Arlene's isn't fancy fare, mostly burgers and wings, but it's Wakpa's favorite watering hole. All small towns need some place for the buying and selling of gossip, and Arlene's is our designated establishment.

"Evening, miss," the man said, turning to me and dipping his head. "Ted Wint."

"Corinne Kaminski," I said. "Oh, hello." This I directed to a woman, presumably Ted's wife, who had just gotten out of the car. She was a round woman with frizzy gray hair wearing a nicely tailored coat and slacks. The lights from the cars set her pair of heavy diamond earrings sparkling.

"Hi, hon, I'm Arlene," she said with a wave and a warm smile, and I was briefly starstruck. This was basically the equivalent of meeting Wakpa royalty.

Introductions out of the way, the men set about taking a look at Joe's truck.

"We hit a deer," Joe explained to Ted. "Big mother—" He shot a look toward us ladies. "Real big sucker."

"Got away, huh?" Ted said, craning his neck this way and that to look into the woods. *That's too bad* was what he really meant. Montana natives aren't shy about bringing home a just-hit deer to dress it, and a lot of guys keep deer tags in their car, just in case. Spit and odds are you'll hit an NRA bumper sticker.

"Well, we'll let them get on with it," Arlene said to me with a flap of her hand. "You look like you need to warm up." She beckoned me towards their car, a red sedan on the older side that looked well-maintained. We both got in, her in the front passenger's side and me in the back.

We watched them through the windshield for a minute in silence, before Arlene turned around to look at me.

"Had a fight?" She laughed when I gave a start. "Oh, hon, sixty years on this fair earth, and thirty of those spent in the bar business, will teach you an awful lot about human beings. You're giving off angry vibes brighter than those hazards."

I squirmed in the seat. Her sitting up front like that looking back at me had me feeling like a kid. "It's not going to work out," I said simply.

"Now you don't have to tell me anything about it…" This with a leading pause. Well, it was only natural; this woman and her husband owned the town's gossip factory.

"Anyway," she said, when it was clear I was staying mum on the subject, "fights happen. That's just the way of things. But we can take you home if you'd like." She gave me a wink. "It'd let you have your storming-off moment. Give him something to think about."

I felt my face reddening. "Oh, that's really all right. My dad's on his way to pick me up." How humiliating; now I was really feeling the little-kid role.

"That'd be Walt Kaminski?"

"That's him."

"Good man. And Joe's a good guy, too," she said, with a nod of her head towards the truck. Man, was I getting tired of hearing that. "I'm sure you two will iron things out. Saw you getting chili dogs a while back… You're such a cute couple."

"Not sure about that," I said in a low voice, then my heart leapt as my savior in the form of twin headlights appeared up ahead.

"And that must be Walt," Arlene said, twisting back around. We got out of the car just as my dad pulled up in his pickup.

You know how they say people look like a lot like their dogs? I'd argue the same thing's true of vehicles. I'm not saying my dad looks like his aging truck per se, but the two of them match really well: big, no-nonsense, and often in a less-than-cleanly state, whether by mud splatters or grease stains. My dad's a machine operator at Pyne Metals, and if he leaves the house in his good jeans and blue flannel shirt you know it's a fancy occasion.

Anyway, his truck might be a bit beat-up, but at least it had never tried to commit suicide by deer. To my eyes, it was as beautiful as Cinderella's enchanted carriage, and my dad's arrival as welcome a sight as Prince Charming.

He hopped out and looked me over, face grave. "Sure you didn't bang your head or nothing?"

"I'm good."

"Good." His gaze shifted to Joe's truck and the empty road. "That's a real shame." The men all shook their heads in glum commiseration, before my dad looked back at me with a silent question, and I gave him a thin-lipped smile that meant, *yes.* I'm sure I looked shaken up.

"Chilly out here," I said, shuffling my feet. "Think we'd better get going."

"Yup," my dad said to me, then with a nod to the others: "Night, everyone."

"Mr. Kaminski, I'll just have a word with Corinne, if you don't mind." All eyes in the group swung over to Joe as I said a fleeting, internal prayer for grace.

"Well," said my dad with a cough, "I'm sure that's fine." The older folks shuffled a little further down the road—guaranteed that Arlene's ears were in full eavesdropping mode—and I turned to Joe.

"What's that?"

"Just think more about what I said. I'm serious, Corinne."

"And I'm serious, too. It's not working for me, Joe. That's

nothing on you, but I'll ask you to respect that."

His eyes darkened. "I'll call you, then. Give you a few days."

If there's one thing I hate, it's people who nod along to what you're saying and don't hear a single word. It seemed this evening had been sent to test me, and I'd at last reached my threshold.

"No," I snapped, "you won't. It's over." I heard the older folks' conversation from behind us go quiet. "Don't call me, don't text me, and don't drop by the *goddamn store*!" And I turned on my heel and marched away to my getaway truck.

Chapter Three

I JUST ABOUT SNARLED AT MY PHONE THE NEXT MORNING WHEN I grabbed for it. It was a mess of text messages. Arlene sure worked fast; I'd have to remember to nominate her for Busybody of the Year Award.

Ray: You good to come in today? Heard about the accident.

Kris: Just heard you and Joe broke up!!!!! I thought you guys were so great together, did he say something to you??

Evan: Out of the Aether was all hype btw, subpar imho

Evan: also I know you were worried about me closing the shop last night but everything went fine

Evan: you guys hit a deer? you ok?

Evan: umm and I just heard you broke up with Joe, you alright?

Molly: omg r u for real

Molly: girl take it back, you guys are like a walking Instagram photo

Molly: corinne

Molly: Corinne! >:(

Molly: CORINNE WTF HAPPENED LAST NIGHT ANSWER ME DAMMIT

All of Wakpa surely knew the events of last night by now. "The fuck?" I said with a shake of my head towards Midge, our dog, who was still curled up on the quilt in a tight, dark ball. She crooked an ear at me before giving a breathy snort and pulling in closer to herself. My human-breakup fallout clearly didn't rate.

I swiped all the texts away to answer later, then shrugged on a bathrobe and trundled downstairs. My dad was in the kitchen slamming cabinets and getting out the forks with as much rattling as possible; this was his daily preamble to making breakfast for the both of us. Who needs an alarm clock when Walter Kaminski is in the house?

He had just added some off-kilter whistling to the clamor (David Bowie's "Starman," maybe?) when he heard me enter the kitchen and paused the commotion. He regarded me carefully for a moment, then went with the safest question.

"Two slices of bacon or three?"

"Two's great, thanks." I stepped around him to turn down the kitchen TV (he always likes to get an eyeful of the weather girl, who was really outdoing herself today in a coral off-shoulder number), then I gave my potted herbs on the windowsill a once-over to see if they needed water. "And thanks for picking me up last night."

We chatted together about this and that as he melted butter in the pan and whisked the eggs, avoiding mention of the night before. One of his hunting buddy's daughters was pregnant with twins, he'd written up Steve yesterday for being late for the nth time—things like that.

"And I'm hoping for an elk later today," he said as he plopped the plates on the table.

"Today's the day?"

"Better be," he said, taking a peek out our dinette picture window at the sky before nodding at the TV. "My girl Amy says just a few light flurries. Maybe a snow squall tomorrow, though."

"Snow squall?"

"I guess all the snow just drops at once. Anyway," he said cheerfully, "that's tomorrow, not today."

"You'll get him," I said as I reached for the bacon. "Just be careful out there."

Dad and I live in an old cozy farmhouse on the edge of a wide meadow. Come summertime the meadow blooms with little red and yellow wildflowers, but it was December now, so all you could see out the picture window was one big swath of pillowy snow. Past the meadow is a stretch of woods, with craggy mountains beyond that that clamber high towards the sky.

The land's ours a good ways out from the meadow, not so far as the mountains, but way, way back into the woods. My great-great-great-granddad came to America from Poland back in 1860-something, heard tell of gold out in Montana, and struck out to find it. Whether he had some talent for prospecting or was just very lucky I'm not sure, but he did end up making a sizable fortune. Family legend says he fell in love twice along the way—first with Montana, then with a woman who'd come west with her late husband. The poor man had been killed in a skirmish with the Sioux, leaving his wife widowed at twenty-one.

So of course my great-great-great-granddad and the young widow got hitched, and he bought a parcel of land for a homestead—land which has stayed in the family ever since. This fact my dad makes sure to remind all his hunter buddies of to no end, since it means the laws are a lot looser when he hunts on our property—hence the quest for an elk, since we were past the season's end by a week or two. This year hadn't been good to my dad hunting-wise, and my dad's good friend, Craig Morrigan, had already used up *his* elk tag, so my dad had been itching to put an end to Craig's boasting.

"And what're your plans for today?" my dad asked, tossing a bit of scrambled egg to Midge, who'd seen fit to join us at last.

"Head in to work soon," I said. It was Saturday, and most Saturdays I worked my usual later shift, but after Joe had bought the movie tickets I'd asked Ray if I could switch my shift around, which meant I'd actually get out of work at a decent time today. "Might ask Molly if she wants to do something." It would be best to get her chiding out of the way sooner rather than later.

We spent the next couple minutes in comfy silence, him sipping his coffee and me my tea. I was chewing on a question, tossing it this way and that in my mind till I decided to just spit it out.

"Do you think it's a bad decision, me splitting up with Joe? Because everyone else seems to think we're perfect together. They think I've lost my mind."

He regarded me over his coffee mug for a moment, then his mustache twitched as he smiled. "You know, your mom and I were a certified odd couple."

"Hm?"

"That's right," he said, eyes sliding away from mine into memory. "She just about glowed when she walked down the street. Just beautiful, and kind, charming, funny… She could have had her pick of anyone—but she chose me." He shook his head before looking back to me. "Of course, a lot of that's down to my own dashing good looks"—he punctuated this with a grin and a wave towards his flannel-clothed paunch—"but even so, she really flummoxed some people. Before we got married, I know a few things were said to her that she didn't see too kindly. Her great aunt, in particular, had a very… misguided conversation with your mom on the eve of our wedding."

My jaw dropped. "I had no idea."

"Well, it didn't bother either of us much, to be honest. We were in love—what'd your mom care about some old lady's opinions? She told the great aunt to get lost, in nicer words, I'm sure.

"So," he said, blowing out a breath, "I'm not saying you have to pick a goof like your old dad. All I mean is that people can get a little bold sometimes about minding other people's business. But"—and here he pointed a finger at me—"you're the one living your life, not them. Joe seemed fine, when he was over at the house that time. I know folks really like him. But I didn't see you… light up around him. So you might think up some choice words to tell your friends. 'Bug off,' is out of style, so's I'm told."

I crooked a smile at him. "Thanks."

"Good luck," he said, sliding a hand across the table to pat my own, before clearing his throat and standing up. "All right, daylight's burning! I'm off in a few."

"Be careful," I told him again. It made me nervous, sometimes, thinking of him out in the woods with just his wits and his gun. A charging grizzly wasn't anything to sniff at.

He grinned and flapped a hand at me. "Yeah, yeah—bug off."

What a relief to go into work on an earlier shift! I was scheduled with Gabriella, our newest college kid and Evan's crush. Gabriella is a snub-nosed girl who likes eyeliner a bit too much, and I couldn't pretend to know her well, but that was for the best; she cared nothing for my romantic life, and she was quite the chatterer, so over the course of the day I heard all the details about the party she'd gone to last night: the girl down the hall's outfit, the jungle juice which had been *so much better* than last time, the boy who might or might not have been flirting with her. (Poor Evan. I'd pretend I hadn't heard anything about it.) It went on and on, pleasant, droning background noise to distract me from the tornado that would soon be touching down.

The tornado called me at three, right as I was grabbing a pencil to update my time sheet.

"Hey," said Molly. "What's up?" Amazing how much meaning you can pack into two syllables: some combination of *how are you?* and *no, really, how ARE you?* and *what the fuck were you thinking?*

"You know," I said, driving the pencil point into the paper until it crumbled into a tiny graphite mound. "Nothing much."

Brief silence on the line. I could feel Her Tornado-ness gathering her forces together, like the Big Bad Wolf getting ready to blow down a house. "You've left me on read since one o'clock." This was true; she'd sent me a long string of increasingly distraught and complicated emojis that I'd flicked away to decipher later. I'm not much for hieroglyphics.

"Yeah, well…" I poked at the graphite mound, smearing it into a little black rainbow.

"Corinne Eleanor Kaminski!" (She huffs.) "Don't you 'yeah, well' me!" (She puffs.) "I am *disturbed* that you think this is a leave-on-read type of relationship!" (And there goes the house.) "Now, you worked with Gabriella today, right? You guys about finished?"

"Mm-hm."

"I'm going to pop by the liquor store, then we're having a night in at your place. Any booze requests?"

I thought for a second. "Just rum for me."

"You getting sick?" She knew me too well.

"Bit of a sore throat, that's all. Took me a while to get to sleep last night."

"All right, then," she said, and I could hear her softening a little. "Rum for you and rosé for me—yum. I've already told Kurt he's going to have to order in; that man couldn't even make DiGiorno, I swear. So you go home, and I'll be there soon, and then we're going to talk."

"Mol, I had to do it."

"I'm sure you did. Tell me all about it soon."

Going off looks alone, Molly wouldn't seem like an intimidating individual; it's hard to achieve that when you're just a few precious inches over five feet, with sky-blue eyes and blond, bobbed hair that curls into natural ringlets. A teeny-tiny Glinda comes to mind.

But if we're talking fey creatures, personality-wise Molly veers much closer to a spitfire Tinker Bell. Half an hour after I got home, I was just peeking out the front window wondering where she was when her car appeared around the bend in our long driveway. She pulled up to the house in a hurry, scattering gravel in her wake, then burst from the car, a brown paper bag tucked under her arm. I opened the door as she marched up the front porch and set the liquor down with a clunk. Then she swept me into a hug that could crush steel beams, before pulling back to look at me. Her eyes were sharp as a military general surveying a map of the troops.

"You haven't been crying. You're not upset about this. You've broken up with him, and it's all in the past already in your mind. Oh God, it really is over." She shook her head at me, curls bouncing furiously. "Corinne, I'm on your side, I always am, but this is a hard one. I had a secret Pinterest board for *your* wedding."

"You know," I said, "you could always have a… a vow renewal ceremony with Kurt or something. Scratch that itch." Molly and her husband had been an item since middle school, broken up for a while after high school to date other people, then gotten back together again and officially tied the knot around a year ago. The wedding had been a cute, slapdash affair—an Internet-ordained officiant, then a potluck in the backyard with beers in a cooler.

She wrinkled her nose at me. "I'm not sixty, Corinne. Also Pinterest dreams are free."

"My dad says I should tell you to mind your own business," I said as we went into the house. I shut the door firmly; it was finally starting to get well and truly cold, and it looked like the promised snow flurries were about to start.

"And is Mr. Kaminski here right now? No? Oh, hey there." Midge had joined us from her spot on the living-room couch and was giving Molly a good sniff. "Because if he's not, then I don't want to hear about it, because as far as I'm concerned you've had a psychotic break. Or maybe entered a—a fugue state, or something." She rooted around for a corkscrew in our catchall kitchen drawer. "I heard them talking about those on the morning show last week."

I laughed. "Stop armchair-psychologizing me."

"Stop needing an armchair psychologist." Finding the corkscrew at last, she set to opening the wine while I got out the eggs from the refrigerator. Tea and chicken broth are for people who like staying sick, and we Kaminskis are made of stronger stuff, that's what my grandma always said, so an oncoming cold called for her much-tested kogel mogel recipe, complete with the requisite, hearty slug of rum. Whisk together some egg yolks and sugar, add the liquor, then raisins or marshmallows if you like raisins or marshmallows, and there you have it. The science was still out on the actual efficacy of the drink, but at least you go into your sickness a lot more cheerful.

"Joe showed up at the shop last night. Didn't tell me, just dropped by," I told her as I hauled out the sugar jar from the pantry.

"Did he?"

"Yeah. Wanted to come by as a surprise, then go to dinner." And I took her through the whole night: Joe's declaration of love, the suggestion to move in together, the accusation of cheating, the deer, Arlene. By the time my tale had wrapped up we'd moved to the couch in the living room. I was through my first drink, Molly was into her second, and Midge was at our feet, in the process of dozing off. I'd given her the leftover egg whites. How sweet: the three of us having a girls' night in, each with our beverage of choice.

"I get it now," Molly said glumly, running her finger along the top of her glass. "Didn't expect that from Joe, but all right. And what about the deer? You doing okay?"

I looked away from the concern in her eyes and shrugged. I'd spent the rest of last night in my own head, watching the deer dash before the car, hearing the cascading sounds of the accident, feeling the car jerk me about like a rag doll. Sleep had only released me from those fun thoughts past two in the morning.

"Yeah," I said simply.

"You could have called out today. I'm sure Ray would have understood."

I looked down at my hands. "He did offer. I'd rather just stay busy."

A moment's pause, then, "Well, okay. So are you on to the next? Kurt's got a cousin you might like. Let me show you a picture." She was already reaching for her phone.

"It's okay," I said, waving my hand for her to put it away. "I think I'll stay off guys for a little while." Like the male sex was some sort of drug—hah! Who needed them? Not this girl. "Real live ones, I mean. I am, however, totally available for some fictional romance." Molly and I have a whole slew of favorite shows for this purpose—the old *Pride and Prejudice* miniseries, *True Blood*. Even some old *Star Trek* episodes have their swoony moments; we're particular to *DS9*.

She grinned broadly and swirled the dregs around in her glass. "All right, your choice."

"Alexander Skarsgård?" Molly and I were forever holding out for Sookie to ditch Bill and get with her much-more-handsome vampire admirer.

"Sure thing." She got to work setting up the TV as I went into the kitchen to top her up and whip together another kogel mogel.

Two episodes later, the night was getting on, and I could just about feel the alcohol seeping from my pores. Molly had moved on from rosé to a peanut-butter sandwich so she could sober up, and Joe was ancient history; vamps all the way, baby.

"Sure you're good to drive?" I asked her when she started making movements to leave halfway through the next episode.

"I'm fine," she said as she traipsed into the kitchen to grab her coat. "But you finish up and text me how this one ends; I don't remember it."

We did our hugs goodbye, and I watched from the porch as she went out to her car.

"Take it slow," I said, a vision of the deer coming to me once more. Ugh.

"Of course. Love you, Cor."

Aww. "Love you, too. Night." Then she was off.

Back in the house, Midge gave me a wide-mouthed yawn, and I nodded at her. "I feel that. Let's go, then."

We went upstairs, and I dragged myself through my night routine—always a trial when you're decently sloshed. Makeup off, teeth cleaned, vitamins taken: check, check, check! We were doing well. I even gave the anthurium on my bedside table a misting; it was starting to look needy.

Then to bed, with my laptop balanced on my stomach and Midge at the foot of the bed, doing her job nicely as designated foot warmer. I made it twenty minutes more into the episode before I caught myself nodding off. Pushing away the laptop, I squished down into my pillow, ready for Mr. Skarsgård to whisk me away to dreamland.

Call it some kind of enchantment woven by the vampires and the alcohol: I hadn't even realized my dad had never come home.

Chapter Four

MIDGE WHINED ME AWAKE AROUND SEVEN THE NEXT MORNING, and as I stumbled down the stairs to let her out I did notice then that the house was too quiet. Dad's a snorer—I'm talking lawnmower levels of loud. And then there's the daily racket in the kitchen once he wakes up. There's no hiding his non-presence.

"Hmm," I said to Midge as she shuffled back into the house, and she looked at me with her solemn eyes as if saying *hmm* right back, before shaking a dusting of snow from her dark fur. That's the way it is in Wakpa; when it's winter it's *winter*, and the days it doesn't out-and-out snow it threatens blizzards and mists snowflakes.

Probably he'd nabbed an elk at last, had taken his time dressing it, then headed over to Craig Morrigan's house to rub it in his face. And since we were going on *probably*s, they'd probably made a night of it, drinking and shit-talking each other, which meant he'd probably stayed the night there. Had my dad's pickup been here when I'd come home from work? I couldn't remember now.

But Dad hadn't texted me to say he planned to stay the night at Craig's, and that was a bit odd now I thought of it, since he usually did tell me he would… in fact, pretty much always did tell me… in fact, had never *not* told me, as best I could recall. My stomach tightened a little, some mixture of nerves and a queasy memory of the kogel mogels, and I quick put on my coat and my snow boots and stomped outside.

Not in the shed, not around back, not anywhere I could see, and his red truck was parked in his usual spot, coated in a thin, even layer of snow. I stared at the pickup for a good few seconds, biting my lip, then trooped back inside and slammed the door. The silence of the house hung heavy like a shroud, and I tried to shake it off, slapping the warmth back into my hands and humming some nonsense tune to myself as I went upstairs to grab my phone, still wearing my snow boots. Midge followed me up, tail wagging, with her disemboweled flamingo toy in her mouth. It leaked puffs of white stuffing after her like a trail of breadcrumbs.

My call to my dad went straight to voicemail. Worry began balling together at the back of my throat, even though I knew going right to voicemail really meant nothing. Dad's not exactly the charge-his-phone-every-night type, or maybe he'd switched it off entirely for yesterday's hunt; I wouldn't put it past him. Anything to bag an elk and show Craig what's what. And so maybe his phone was off, and he'd come home last night after I'd turned in, and I hadn't noticed, and then he'd gone out earlier this morning. Somewhere. Without his truck.

The door would slam downstairs in a second or two, and eve-rything would be right as rain.

And all that made sense to my brain in a logic-ey way—the sensible things well-intentioned people tell you when you lay your worries out on the table, coupled with a pat on the hand and a *there, there, don't you worry*. But logic's a featherweight when it's up against fear, and the knot in my throat was heavy as a marble now.

This wasn't right. He should be here, the two of us squabbling over the last piece of bacon. I shifted back and forth, scritched Midge on the head, then went back downstairs to call Craig.

Craig Morrigan's a good guy, but he's Dad's friend, not mine, so I didn't have him as a contact in my phone. Yet the face of our refrigerator houses a collection of age-old wisdom to rival the Dead Sea Scrolls, and I quickly located his number on a yel-lowed, curling list of names and numbers marked *Emergency*.

"*Hyel*-lo," Craig shouted into the phone when he answered, because that's who Craig is, big belly, big smile, big laugh. Just big all the way. Get him and my dad in the same room together and you'll just about go deaf, the both of them booming jokes and jabs at each other like auditory bombs.

"Craig!" I yelled, since once one person's shouting it's in-stinct to shout back, and the nerves were crawling all over me at this point, besides. "It's Corinne!"

"Corinne! Well, that's a surprise! How're you doing these days? I heard you and Joe… Well, how are you?"

"I'm… Uh, listen, Craig, it's my dad. He's not… with you? Over there?"

A pause, during which the word *bear* throbbed through my brain like a heartbeat. "Well, no," Craig said, "he's not." *Bear.* "Haven't seen him since Friday." *Bear.* "You all right?" *Bear, bear, bear.*

"Yeah. No. He's not here, and he went out hunting yesterday, and I'm... um..."

Craig's voice swooped in like Superman before the pause grew too long. "He's fine, Corinne."

"Yeah?"

"Listen, love, I'm sure he just went out for a walk. Something like that. He'll be back."

"Right. Yeah, I'm sure that's it."

"You want me to come on by?"

"No, no, that's fine. Thanks, Craig."

"Sure?"

"Yeah. Thanks. I'll call you again in a bit if he's still not back."

I hung up, wondering if I was stupid telling Craig not to come, feeling I probably was. But there wasn't anything wrong, was there? My dad just... wasn't here.

The silence pressed down on my ears. Midge whined, the flamingo on the floor beside her, its white guts leaking out. *Bear, bear, bear.*

I blew out a quick breath, rocked forward on my toes, looked at the front door, willed it to open. It did not.

"Just a quick little walk," I said to Midge, and her ears perked up at the *W* word.

It wasn't a sensible thing to do. The sensible thing would have been to call Craig back, to tell him to get down here, make him make it all right. But strangeness was in the air, and I was under its sway, like a guppy being swept downstream a river.

Leaving a scrawled post-it note on the door for Dad—*Going out for a walk with Midge, CALL ME!!*—I stepped out of the warmth of our house into the chill winter air. Midge was at my side, clad in her winter coat and dog booties, and I had one of my dad's rifles in a sling on my back. I'd noted with a sinking feeling as I picked the gun from his collection that his favorite one of the bunch was absent, along with his usual winter gear.

We paused there in front of the door, looking out across the meadow, glistening arsenic white in the early morning sunshine. Midge took a long, deep sniff, scenting the mountain air, and I gazed onward, my eyes roaming the woods and peaks.

I sucked in a crisp breath and cleared my throat. "Dad?!" The cry was too high and shaky, too tempting of fate. Steeling myself, I started across the meadow, then opened my mouth again. My voice came stronger this time. "Hello, Dad?!" The call evaporated away into the air the instant it left my lips, leaving a vacuum of stillness in its wake. Wind. A bird twittered. No answer.

So I kept my pace steady across the meadow, feeling the distance between myself and the house stretch thinner with every step. My dad had to be out here, somewhere. But somewhere could be anywhere, and I was just one person amongst the sprawling press of wilderness. Where should I even begin? Indecision slowed my footsteps as I combed my memory for an answer. Hunting's not really my hobby, but I'd gone out with my dad occasionally when I was younger. One of his tree stands out east, maybe? But bull elk are wily, their roaming patterns unpredictable, so probably my dad had opted for still-hunting—the hunter's slow, silent version of hide-and-seek. That meant woods with decent cover, especially woods with a lot of aspen for elk to munch on.

West it was.

We hit the tree line, and I called out for him again, startling the birds into silence. Midge trotted along cheerfully beside me, never straying far as she went about her dogly duty of cataloging all the smells. She's a black, forty-pound mutt, with a sheepdog's smarts and a retriever's patience, never the kind to lose her head over a rabbit. She'd signal me if she noticed something particular, that I was sure of.

We reached the aspen grove before long, and I checked the time—scarcely twenty minutes since we'd set out.

The elk had been gnawing at the trees, that much was obvious; black, furrowed bites scored the paper-thin bark. I turned around in a slow circle, and Midge began snuffling through the underbrush. There was no one around, save for a squirrel chittering at us from a tree branch, and it was just a squirrel, but its chiding and my tremulous calling for my dad and the absolute absence of any other soul all mushed together in a way where I began to feel very foolish. I had no idea where to go from here; it wasn't like I had a map of the woods tattooed in my mind, so that meant heading home—where, I told myself firmly, Dad was certain to be, since his absence had nothing to do with a hunting mishap. And I should have listened to Craig instead of letting my nerves whip me into a panic, since now I'd have to make my way home and feel like an idiot when Dad was there. And then this would become one of those memories, terrible in the moment but funny in retrospect. I set my shoulders and made to turn around towards home.

Midge yipped. She was standing by a cluster of bushes twenty feet away or so, and her spine was ramrod straight, her tail still. I felt myself move toward her, like a conveyor belt was shuttling me onward rather than my own legs. My brain was a low buzz.

An outstretched arm on the ground, poking out from behind the knotty tangle of undergrowth, almost invisible because it was covered in snow camo.

I drifted closer, and the world around me grew cold and distant. Yes, there he was, I could see him now that I was around the thicket. No marks on him, not a scratch; he lay on the ground like he was taking a nap in the snow, his rifle beside him.

On my knees now, gasping, nonsense words in my mouth as I scrabbled at his face, at his coat. And Midge was crowding in toward my face, eyes wide with concern, not even looking at him, like she already knew the score. I pushed her away roughly and clung to him, ripping off his glove, fumbling for his hand. Cold.

He was gone.

Chapter Five

THERE, CLUTCHING HIM IN THE SNOW, TIME LEFT ME. THE world shrunk down, one small spotlight on a dark stage, leaving me in a bubble with just my father and my grief for company.

Crying, pleading, crying some more. The beads of my tears forming a sorry pattern on his coat. Desperate whispers on my lips, all the things you want to tell a person before they go—but he'd left before I'd had the chance.

A whispery whine from Midge brought me back, slowly, to myself. She was huddled in close to me, little shivers shaking her body. We had to get back; the temperature felt like it had dropped a good ten degrees, and the wind had picked up, stirring the trees around us into a creaking fervor. A pinprick of cold stung my cheeks; it was starting to snow.

I cast a look around the grove in vain for something to cover him. There was nothing, of course. "I'll come back," I murmured to him, my voice low and soft from crying. I couldn't take him with me; I'm a hundred and twenty pounds soaking wet, and my dad was easily twice that. Brushing a few stray snowflakes from his coat, I stood up, gave him one long, last look, then turned away and started home.

The world was a blur around me as I walked. The word *alone* churned within me, the two syllables sickening. It had been just us since Mom had died, our fierce family of two always perfectly enough. What was I to do without him? My breath caught, and I sagged against a nearby tree, sobs racking my body.

After a few minutes my tears ceased again, the wind stepping in, mother-like, to dry my cheeks. "All right," I said to Midge (and more than a little to myself). I pushed off the tree trunk. "Let's… let's go."

As I walked on, my loss a deep ache, I vaguely registered that the temperature had dropped once more. The snow thickened into a churning mass of white, as if God were shaking the world up like a snow globe, and my footsteps slowed, halted.

The snow on the ground before me was fresh and untrampled. This wasn't right; I'd been retracing my tracks home. Lost in my own mind, I'd lost the path as well. Stupid.

I turned around in a circle. The air was heavy with snow, every direction the same somber gray trees. What was it Dad had said yesterday? A snow squall. *All the snow just drops at once.*

"We'll head back," I said to glum-faced Midge, about-facing.

But after just a few minutes I halted again. The snow, heavy and furious, had smoothed my previous footprints into nonexistence.

That was when I fished my phone from my snow-sodden coat pocket. That was when I discovered that in last night's kogel-mogel-induced sleepiness I had neglected to charge my phone; the battery symbol was lit up a worrying crimson. *4%.* I may be blessed with my mother's good looks and a good many other things, as my dad is wont to tell me, but in this way I am unfortunately my father's daughter. Midge gave a little whimper, and I pushed my tongue to the roof of my mouth, trying to dam up the fear.

I opened up my GPS app, my gloved fingers stinging from the cold. *3%.* We were somewhere west of the house—northwest, if I had to guess. All I needed was a proper heading southeast, and we'd be okay. I tapped in our address, sending a silent prayer up to the satellites on high.

The app found us immediately, the blue *you-are-here* dot never a more welcome sight. My stomach, which had been doing acrobatic flips, settled a little. I took a few steps, altering our heading—to the complete opposite direction I would have picked, so praise be to the tech gods—and set off.

But after twenty seconds I heard a cheerful ding that turned me to ice. The app was readjusting, my little blue dot skipping way up north for a few seconds, then zooming southwest.

The mountains were messing with the signal. It was anyone's guess where we actually were.

2%.

"Work," I pleaded, holding the phone aloft, trying to snare a signal to keep us from freezing to death out here.

1%. The screen dimmed, the map almost imperceptible. The blue dot darted east, then north—then held. And held even longer, for five, ten, fifteen seconds, as I held my breath alongside it.

"All right," I said with an exhale, my breath a thick white cloud. I started forward hesitantly, ready for a ding that didn't come, even after twenty paces. We would make it home after all. We would escape this rising snowstorm, and life would continue—a strange, sorrowful life without my dad, but at least we would find our way ho—

Ding. The app was recalculating again, the blue dot jittering south, then west...

The screen died, reflecting a dark reflection of my panicked face back at me.

I pressed the power button frantically, willing the phone to find more juice, knowing it didn't work like that. And hadn't Dad always railed about trusting new-fangled technology with tasks that all the old ways accomplished just as well, and here I was, his very own daughter, venturing into the woods with a rifle, ready to take potshots at bears, but she *hadn't thought to bring a compass.* He would have shouted me senseless, and I bit back a sob, wishing he *could* be here to do just that, wishing this whole day could start again and I would wake up and there he'd be, calling me downstairs for eggs.

We were going to die out here.

In my peripheral vision, I could see Midge making plaintive eyes at me. I slowly spun around, trying to pick the worthiest direction. All of it looked the same—no recognizable land-marks, just anonymous trees, swirling snowflakes, and the leer-ing promise of death everywhere I looked.

I wavered. Midge shivered again. With a wrenching feeling, I opted for a direction that looked just the same as the rest, feeling as soon as I started walking that I'd chosen wrong. But random chance was all I had left; all visibility was shot in the blizzard.

The going was hard. At every turn, thorny bushes and clusters of fir trees obstructed my path. Snow-laden underbrush caught at my ankles, trying to trip me. The moan of the wind, the creak of the trees, and the crystalline rustle of falling snowflakes twined together into an eerie cacophony. Soon the wind was against us; I leaned into it, and it snatched the breath out of my lungs, setting me gasping.

Midge was doing her best, not uttering a peep, but from the hunch of her back I could tell she was miserable. I'd outfitted her in dog booties and her bottle-green winter coat, of course, but there was only so much you could do about a Montana snowstorm, and she didn't have the thickest fur. I wouldn't have brought her with me if I'd known that we… if I'd known. After a little while I bent down and gathered all forty pounds of her up in my arms. She huffed a warm breath in my ear and licked my cheek.

"Sorry," I murmured to her, hugging her in close as the tears welled up again. "I'm so sorry."

With her in my arms, I started forward once more, my footsteps all the slower from her weight. Maybe it would be best to search for some place to hunker down and wait out the storm. If I found a suitable tree, I could clear out a little hovel in the snow and—

Midge gave a sudden cry, her whole body tensing. With a furious wriggle she leapt from my arms to the ground, hackles raised high in a dark, wiry line down her spine.

"Midge!" I cried, starting forward. "Are you—?"

Yet the hot prick of tiny sparks washed over my body, accompanied by a flash of dazzling white-violet. Blinded, I stumbled and loosed a yell, my ankle turning painfully inward. Arms pinwheeling uselessly, I pitched face forward into the snow, feeling the needle-sharp tip of a twig scratch me just below the eye as I fell.

I rolled over and spat out a mouthful of snow. The world was a whitewash of light, like a million flashbulbs had all gone off at once. Fresh panic seethed within me. I couldn't see. *I COULDN'T SEE.*

Something wet bumped my cheek: Midge's nose. "H-hey there," I said, sitting up and hugging her tight around the neck.

A female voice, flat and dispassionate, said... *something.* What sounded like a lot of *R*s all mushed together—not any language I knew.

"Hello?" I scrambled back a pace as Midge loosed a low warning growl. "Who's there?"

And the woman spoke again, another mashed-up string of syllables. She sounded close, but... above me somehow? Up a tree? I blinked my eyes furiously, trying to clear the blindness, but the brilliant white light that had replaced my vision refused to dissipate.

"Wh-who's there? You speak English?"

More unintelligible words—what language even *was* that?—then silence.

I took a few tentative steps forward, arms outthrust to keep from blundering into anything—or anyone. Something brushed my calf, and I yelped, only to realize it was Midge.

Slowly, the white in my eyes seeped away. Ghostly silhouettes of trees melted in around me. I cast a shaky look around for the female speaker, still clutching the rifle tight, but she was nowhere to be seen. A few paces ahead of me, Midge had her nose thrust into the snow as she inhaled a scent.

Then I frowned, blinked, seeing the landscape before me clearer, now that my vision was coming back to normal. We were in a semi-clearing, the lay of the land fairly flat. Yet the white ground between the sparse trees had none of the smoothness of fresh-laid snow, but was marred with ripples and mounds and whorls, like some force from above had carved the snow into strange, alien beauty.

And as I cast a puzzled gaze around me, I noticed that ten feet to my right, in the direction I'd come from, the air was clogged with snowflakes—yet here where I stood, there were no snowflakes falling anymore. Vaguely, I thought of the sudden silence when you drive under an overpass in heavy rain.

Midge gave a sharp snort and lifted her nose from the snow, scenting the air.

The woman spoke again from somewhere above me—a blurt of words, which then slowed. *"Ix... zver... ahlm... ish..."*

I looked up... all the way up.

A silent, sparkling vortex hung above me sixty or so feet in the air, a sprawling black hole smack dab in the middle of the sky. And like a movie projected onto a screen, I could see the blizzarding sky *over* the vortex, the two overlaid images clashing dizzyingly.

I staggered in the snow, nearly falling. I was shaking, a few gasps escaping my lips, and Midge had raised her head in a crooning howl, straight up towards the dark, spinning hole.

"Nae… morun… zeer," the woman finished, her countdown over—for of course she was counting, counting *down*, and I knew then with all certainty that something terrible and unnatural had taken my father's life—not a heart attack or a stroke, but something entirely foreign to this world.

And that thing was about to happen to me, too. I threw myself towards Midge, but too late, too late, I was lifting off the ground, a force from above siphoning me up into the heavens.

Chapter Six

THE ABDUCTION FELT AWFUL—A SORT OF BATTERING, WINDY pressure, as if I were a speck of dust being drawn up a vacuum chute. The air had a soupy thickness to it as it buoyed me upwards. I've never been fond of heights, but I couldn't help a glance downward; the ground spun below me like I was in a fun house. A chorus of yelps rang out; Midge was a few yards to my left, being buffeted around in thin air just like me. She writhed, eyes wide with panic.

I looked upward once more. I was near enough to the vortex now that it filled my vision, blotting out the sky. No denying that this was a beautiful way to die, looking into this beckoning, unknowable darkness. If only there wasn't this ever-building pressure, which was moving from discomfort to real pain now...

I screamed, and the wind tore my breath from my throat.

Up and up and up. The darkness welcomed me, enfolded me. I closed my eyes. *You weren't wrong about the odds, Evan. All it takes is one.*

And I landed in a heap on a cool, hard floor. The chaos of winds was gone, utter stillness taking its place. I waited for one long moment, drenched and utterly exhausted, like a butterfly that's just escaped the prison of its cocoon. In a second some creature's slick, amphibious hand would surely reach out and paw at me. They'd strap me to a gurney and wheel me to a blindingly white room, ready to commence testing. A glistening array of sharp instruments… the looming threat of probing… I'd seen this movie before.

Nothing—the room remained still and quiet. Slowly, I slid my hands under my shoulders, pushing up from the floor with a groan. Every part of me ached.

A sudden weight smacked me back down, like an anvil had fallen from above. I cried out, balling up instinctively, only to hear the unmistakable click of frantic claws on a slippery floor.

"Midge!"

I sat up and opened my arms to her, and she leaped into them, tail wagging madly. Her dark eyes bulged, showing the whites. As she nuzzled into me, giving my neck a tongue-washing, I peeled off my gloves and threw them to the floor. Flexing my fingers to bring warmth back into them, I rose to my feet with a wince, swung the rifle forward, and took stock of my surroundings.

I'd landed in a small, square room not much bigger than a closet. I wrinkled my nose; a sterile, hospital-like smell floated in the air, like the room had recently been cleaned. The floor was crafted from some neutral material, not quite plastic, not quite stone, and polished to a smooth shine—*the better for washing away blood, my dear*. A dull hum of power vibrated through the floor.

The walls were… well, I'd never seen anything like them. They were awash with colorful fractals, mostly varying shades of red, with offshoot specks of fiery orange, like sparks from a fire—and the fractals were *moving*, in a sort of languid, lazy way. I reached out a trembling hand to brush the wall, only to draw back when a little cluster of orange flecks sped toward my fingertips. It—whatever *it* was—knew I was here.

Neck protesting, I turned my head upwards. A large, glowing orb in one corner suffused the room with a rosy light. Embedded in the middle of the ceiling was a complicated, circular piece of machinery, its interior a shadowed hole. A high-tech version of a garbage chute, if I had to guess—a garbage chute that had unceremoniously dumped me and my dog on the floor. Maybe if I could find something to stand on, I could pull myself back up into the chute? But then there was the issue of Midge…

I looked back to the walls; the red fractals were still moving sluggishly. And I saw then something that I hadn't noticed on first inspection: a crisp seam down the middle of the wall to my left, with a small silver button to the side. A burble of shocked laughter escaped my lips. It was all too familiar.

A door. Had to be.

I eyed it leerily, heart hammering a quick beat against my rib cage. One option was to just stay here, waiting for the inevitable entrance of God-knows-what horror. Yet shock and grief and adrenaline had knitted themselves together into a raw, pulsing nerve within me that itched to Do Something. I'm not a violent person—I've been known to rescue window-concussed robins and worms that have beached themselves on the sidewalk—but here, at what was surely the end of my life, the solid weight of the rifle felt like just the right kind of medicine. Go down swinging and all that.

Midge seemed to be having similar ideas; she was burying her nose in the seam of the door, giving it a long, hard sniff.

"One last walk?" I whispered to her, sidling closer to the button.

She looked at me, eyes intent and luminous, and I took that as assent. Checking that the rifle's safety was off, I flattened myself to the wall—more orange sparks, ugh—hit the button, and shivered as the door whisked open.

Silence from outside. I slowly peeked my head out; a dim, empty hallway lay beyond. The light filtering out from our little room lit both sides of the corridor only faintly. Still, I could see more fractals crawling over the walls. Shadows clung thickly to the end of the hall.

Hssss. The door slid shut again, nearly smacking me in the face, and I jumped about ten feet. That I hadn't pulled the trigger was a miracle worthy of sainthood.

I jabbed the button again. When the door opened once more, I took a deep breath, squared my shoulders, and stepped out into the darkness, Midge by my side.

I half-expected a siren to start blaring, perhaps for the corridor to come to life with red alarm lights. Instead, there was a faint click, and a spotlight split the shadows; an unlit orb light on the ceiling, twin to the one in the room behind us, had just flicked on.

Motion detection—but the kind of tech that behaved indiscriminately, whether it was sensing human, canine, or… *other*. I took a few more steps forward, and another orb light further down the hallway sprang to attention.

And now that I could see everything better, a curious feeling crested over me, for there was a beauty here—a strange beauty, yes, but beauty nonetheless. There was something foreign, something off-puttingly not *human*, about the very construction of the hallway. Maybe the height of the ceiling, or perhaps the way the ceiling and walls joined at the seams—right angles like you'd see anywhere, but something was different all the same.

The air, too, smelled different—tasted different! Not stale or thick or acrid. Breathable, thank God. Just a faint, ineffable otherness.

And more of those fractals spilled over everything, little flashes of silver and peachy-gold surfacing sometimes through the red, the patterns florid and curling. I'd never been to Versailles, but I'd seen photographs, and that was what I thought of now. I could just envision some lithe alien princess floating down this corridor, the very picture of beauty amongst her otherworldly rococo palace.

Midge, meanwhile, had moved on down the hallway, in full-on sniffing mode at this point. What, I wondered, did aliens smell like? A kind of sharp, rotting stink, maybe, if they were the spewing-acid-from-their-jaws variety? Or for the classic, dark-eyed, bobble-head type, perhaps a metallic, salt-laced odor?

However they smelled, my puny human nose wasn't picking

up anything besides the slight strangeness of the air, but Midge was hard at work with her nose to the ground, her paws leaving damp prints on the floor.

I followed her. The pattern of the walls seemed to move with me, just the slightest bit more ornate in the area around me than the space I'd just left. I had the sudden, humbling feeling of being inside something alive and much bigger than me and absolutely unknowable. Jonah and the whale. I'd been swallowed alive. And probably because I was in shock—or, even more likely, some place beyond shock—a nervous thrill quivered in my chest, and the old tale of my great-great-great-granddad popped into my head. Is this how he'd felt, looking out across the uncharted fastness of the mountains? *You are the first person to lay eyes on this.*

I kept on walking, around a corner, coming now to another door, complete with its own silvery button. I traced a finger down the seam of the door as Midge padded over to me. What lay beyond it? Discovery by whatever lived on this ship? Then a long, protracted, painful death?

In the end I could either keep exploring or wait around to be found. It wasn't like I'd seen any windows to make a quiet escape—who knew if there was even any place to escape *to*? All bets were off now that I'd traveled through the vortex; for all I knew, it had been a wormhole that had sucked me away to some other planet, entire galaxies removed from Earth.

So I pushed the button, then gripped the rifle tightly as the door hissed open.

I was greeted by a warm blast of humid air, mixed with the

unmistakable scent of greenery. A dim, dense rainforest lay beyond, a white stone path meandering through the middle of it. Jaw hanging open, I stepped through the door, Midge right beside me. I gave a little start when the door shut behind me a moment later.

We were surrounded on all sides by jungle—but a jungle unlike any other. Trees with thick, dark trunks soared high, knots in the bark oozing phosphorescent sap. Their leaves were all shades of reddish purple, and they formed a rosy canopy overhead. Meager knives of light sliced through the leaves, illuminating patches of the forest below: creeping vines, violet undergrowth, flowers with translucent, spiky petals. Thick, red moss coated the ground like a carpet, its blotchy expanse interrupted every so often by squat, blue, jelly-like growths that reminded me of toadstools.

I tipped my head upwards and squinted. I could just barely see a bit of ceiling through the trees; wild as this space felt, we were still indoors. So this was a sort of greenhouse, then.

Redhouse.

Pull yourself together, Corinne.

Was it better to head back into the hallway? Or should I take the path, which cut through the jungle like a clean, white ribbon? I wavered for a moment, then started forward, curiosity getting the best of me.

Trees everywhere pressed in close, like dark enemies leering from either side. Thorny vines draped like streamers from tree to tree, making the path an obstacle course. My light footsteps were the only sound—no bird calls, no screaming insects.

Until I heard voices in conversation. My heart stopped. The sound was distant, the barest, muffled echo, but... voices nonetheless, and one particular voice that I knew—that I'd thought I'd never hear again.

And I'd seen my dad in the clearing, clung to him, pleaded with him to return to me... but maybe I'd seen wrong. My pace quickened. Maybe he'd somehow still been alive, even though I'd felt his nonexistent pulse, seen the non-rise of his chest. The cadence of the words, the low rumble of a voice just barely heard...

But it was my dad's voice; I was certain of it.

I sped down the path, dodging hanging vines and encroaching brambles, Midge at my heels. The path veered left, right, left again... A gazebo-like structure loomed into view, the architecture almost grotesquely ornate; with a quick glance I saw it was empty and hurried on.

The path doubled back... took a swooping right around a stagnant pool, the red algae floating on the surface lending it a sanguine appearance.

And at last, with one final turn, the thick rainforest gave way to reveal a fractal-bedecked wall, the path leading straight to another door; I'd made it to the other side. There was another burst of conversation, filtering to me through the door, and I stabbed at the button to open it. As soon as the wall parted I plunged on through, gun at the ready, leaving the silent eeriness of the jungle behind.

We were in another dim hallway, much like the first, but this one lined with more doors. I heard the voices again, louder this time. That was him; I'd know his deep grumble anywhere. The other speaker was familiar too: that aloof female voice that had performed the countdown. Midge darted ahead of me, ears pricked forward and tail wagging. "Dad?" I called, the rifle shaking in my hands.

"*CORINNE?!*"

It was his voice, sure as I knew anything. "Dad, say something!"

"You need to go!"

"I'm coming for you! Keep talking!" I was getting closer, our game of Marco Polo leading me to him. Midge was pawing at a door up ahead, tail wagging madly.

"Corinne, please! You have to—!"

I punched at the door button and ran through. There he was, standing in the middle of a small, sparse room lit with red lights. A cry ripped from my throat, and I rushed toward him, only to find myself on the floor a second later, having run head-long into… something. Not anything hard, but like I'd been bounced backward by a repelling magnet. And as I shook my head and gathered myself up from the floor, I saw now that the room was not lit up red, but that a plane of crimson light from floor to ceiling divided him from me.

A jail cell. There was no one else in the room—who had he been talking to? I drew nearer to the red light; it hummed as I got closer.

He looked worse for wear, his graying beard a frizzled mess, his face haggard. He was in his usual winter hunting gear: sturdy boots, white camo parka and pants. I'd wet that coat with tears little more than an hour ago, and now here it was and here *he* was again.

"Dad? D-did they hurt you?"

His eyes were panicked. "Get out of here!" Midge let out a high whine at his tone. "Honey, you have to hide—please!"

I ignored him, scanning the room for something, *anything*, to deactivate the wall of light hemming him in. Yet the room was entirely bare, save for more of those slowly writhing fractals.

I turned back to him. "I'm going to find a way to break you out. I'll be back soon."

"No!" His voice dropped to a gruff murmur. "Corinne, listen to me. You came alone?"

"Yes? Well, Midge, but—"

"And no one knows you're here? No one's seen you?"

"No one does. Dad, I saw your body in the forest. You were *dead*, I thought."

"Never mind that." He shot a look at the wall. "There can't be two of us here. But if no one knows—and she might not. She hasn't been speaking English since—"

"Wh-who is she? Who were you talking to?"

"The *ship*, Corinne." I'd never seen him so frantic. "You can't be here. *You have to hide*. Because having two of us on board—"

But the hiss of the door opening cut him off. My dad's eyes widened as they refocused on something behind me... something taller than me. A deep shadow split the room in two. I turned and recoiled.

A monstrous figure stood silhouetted in the doorway. Two lean, muscular legs supported a hulking torso. Powerful shoulders led into a short, thick neck, upon which sat a large head.

There were two eyes where they were supposed to be, a nose, a mouth—clearly evolution on the being's home planet had taken a similar course to humans. Its skin was covered in short, ruddy fur, and in what felt like the barest nod to tameness, the lower half of its body was clothed in plain black pants that ended at the knee. The creature was flat-footed like a human, and it wore dark shoes that looked to be little thicker than socks. As for the top half, a wide, gray-brown strap of knobbly woven fabric ran crosswise from its shoulder to hip, like a somber version of a Miss America sash. Muscles rippled beneath the odd outfit, and I was reminded of a pet stuffed unwillingly into an outfit by its vexing owner.

It looked upon me with a calculating stillness, an all-seeing predator gazing at prey, before it closed the distance between us with one quick stride. Midge loosed a grating bark and jumped before me, hackles high, and I gave a yelp and fell back a step. A dry heat from the wall sparked against the back of my neck. There was no place to run.

"Who are you?" The creature's voice was a low rumble that seemed to quiver in the air. The accent was strange—the *R* a bit too strong, the vowels held a hair too long—but its English was still quite comprehensible. Midge growled.

"I-I..." My wits had scattered to the wind. The creature's baleful eyes, though, held mine with a dizzying focus.

"Quickly!"

That was the last straw for Midge, who launched forward with fangs bared, and that was just the prompt I needed, like a director calling "Action!" at the start of a scene—for there was an obvious solution to this situation. I swung the rifle forward, which I, prime idiot, had been clutching uselessly in those initial shocked seconds of seeing my very first extraterrestrial.

But neither Midge nor I were quick enough. A clawed hand whipped out and plucked the gun from my hands, lifting the sling up and over my head in one quick motion. In the same breath, the creature caught Midge with its other arm and gathered her up in a snarling ball, then opened the door and hurled both her and the rifle into the hallway. Another punch to the door button and my only ally and weapon were locked outside.

"Your name!" it prompted again.

Looking up at this looming, alien thing, I had all rights to be scared out of my mind. That would have been the sensible way to feel. And yes, I was scared, but not terrified—or maybe I'd been terrified for half a second, then crossed beyond that emotion into a prey animal's grim acceptance of the end being nigh.

"M-my name..." Midge was howling outside. The sound made it hard to form sentences.

A thought occurred: divulging any more information than need be didn't seem wise.

Another good idea (I was just full of them, I guess): it wouldn't do to die cowering. I straightened my spine.

"Maybe simple," the creature said at last when the silence grew overlong. Then I swear to God it growled at me. Or at least it said a word that sounded very much like *grrr*. That was followed by a *much* ruder word in English—I couldn't have heard that correctly, could I?—then a sentence or two in its own language. The walls sparkled faintly with orange, like the world's saddest firework. An unseen woman responded coolly, and the creature *grrr*'ed again before shifting its gaze to my dad.

"You know her? She's someone to you, yes? A daughter? A relation?"

"You'll leave her alone and let her go!" shouted my dad.

"Yes," he responded—for the thing—creature—alien clearly fell on the masculine side of the equation; I could see that now. "She'll be leaving immediately."

Every scrap of breath left my lungs. The alien couldn't really mean that—that I would just be going on my merry way. It couldn't be that simple.

No weapon… no recourse of any kind…

I strode over to the alien, quick as I could before I lost my nerve, and swept my hand up—way up—to slap him across the face.

In the moment that followed, everything stood frozen, like a photographer of old's flashbulb had gone off to capture some watershed historical moment. He gaped down at me, his face clearly registering shock. I'd moved from possible imbecile to person of interest. My dad was absolutely silent behind me, no doubt from horror, and I… I couldn't hold my tongue any longer, stupid as it might be.

"I'm Corinne Kaminski. This is my father." No stuttering there; good job, me.

"Your father," the alien repeated, his voice a bare, furious rumble.

"Yes," I said, choking down nerves. I would have given any-thing to look away, but I held the alien's brutish gaze—and searched his face for any trace of humanity.

He was heavy-browed, with a wide, flat nose. The short fur covering his face and the dark mane of hair tumbling wild over his broad shoulders gave a vaguely leonine effect. The alien's two sharp eyes, I saw now, were rimmed thinly with a band of vermilion. They did not stray from my own for a second.

No, there was no humanity in this face. But that didn't mean there wasn't some shred of compassion lurking within.

"And I've come to take him home," I continued. "You said I could leave, so why not the both of us? Why do you care?"

The alien gave a low growl. The tang of adrenaline filled my mouth.

"Your request is impossible," he said at last. "And you'll be going now. Along with your…" One clawed finger crooked behind us toward the door. Midge was still howling.

"Dog?"

"Yes. That. Say your goodbyes."

I shrank back into the corner. "Please!"

His brow creased into a deep glower. "This isn't negotiable. Your father must stay here."

I stole a desperate look at my dad, who was shaking his head at me furiously, eyes glassy. *Memorize the little things*, whispered a sorry voice in my mind. *His face, his eyes. You thought you'd missed your last chance—well, this is the real one.*

Then from deep within me rushed another hot wave of rage that drowned that small voice. I'd lost my father once already today. I wasn't going to lose him again.

"*Why?*" I asked, rounding on the alien. "Why him? And why let *me* go?"

He cast another glance toward the wall. "There's no time for these questions. Say your farewell to him."

It was an absolute dodge of an answer… but I'd gotten an answer all the same, for something in the alien's expression had shifted, blaring at me as familiar. Pity, it seemed, was an interstellar emotion.

"I'll stay here with him, then," I said, swallowing hard.

"No." His voice broached no discussion or compromises.

Why this flat refusal? And in answer, my dad's words rang through my mind.

There can't be two of us here.

"Then—take me instead of him." The words seemed to come from beyond me, from somebody else's mouth.

Dimly, I heard a horrified gasp from behind me. But all my attention was on the alien, who stood statue-still. Flabbergasted, maybe, though the foreign planes of his face offered few clues.

"Please," I said. Was he going to make me beg for this on my hands and knees? "Let me stay in his place."

The alien's gaze bored into me. "You would do that, for him?"

"I-I would. I will."

"And you won't be allowed to return home. You do understand that? This will be your new home until other accommodations can be made."

"Fine." I jutted my chin upward—a veneer of bravery. The word was ash in my mouth.

The alien's red eyes held mine for a second longer, before his focus shifted to the side of the room yet again. He sank into another sharp back-and-forth with the lady in the wall.

My dad, meanwhile, was whispering things to me. I had to reconsider. I couldn't throw my life away like this. And I nodded and cried softly and whispered back that I loved him, but my ear was trained on the alien's conversation. He and the female voice spoke for a moment more, before both fell silent. Then, from the alien: "So you will stay." This with a grunt in my direction. "But he must leave, *now*."

My dad loosed a roar of outrage, and his cry pierced through me, a sound I would never be able to scrub from my memory. "You can't! I won't let you—!"

But the wall of light keeping him from me blinked out. With one swift movement, the alien shoved me towards the far end of the room, even as he grabbed at my dad's coat and tugged him towards the door. Back up went the wall of light, now imprisoning me instead of my dad, our positions reversed in the space of one breath.

My brain struggled to catch up. No, he wouldn't take my dad away without letting me say goodbye, would he? He'd offered time for farewells before. He couldn't—

He could. The door opened at his touch, letting Midge bound back into the room. The alien turned, snarled something unintelligible in her direction, then swept away with my dad in tow, leaving us alone in the holding cell.

Chapter Seven

I'D ASSUMED THAT THE ALIEN WOULD BE BACK FOR ME SOON enough, but after a long while spent watching the door, it was clear he was preoccupied with something else. Not that his human prisoner might need food, water, clothes that weren't soaked through from a snowstorm—no, my basic needs were clearly of no importance. At least the room was decently warm.

It was enough time alone for all my righteous anger to burn away, replaced with a sadness that deepened by the second. My little cell was entirely bare, without even a chair to sit on, so I huddled in a corner, knees to my chest, and let my thoughts descend into misery. To lose your family, your friends, your home, your *planet* in the span of one moment… it was too much. The loss hadn't properly registered yet, but I could feel it lurking on the horizon. Once it hit me, there wouldn't be time enough in a lifetime to mourn the loss.

At least I still had Midge, I thought, trying to rationalize. Things weren't all that bad; if I could just keep telling myself that, eventually I might believe the lie. So I would concentrate right now on the little problems to distract myself from being ripped from my life in one fell swoop. Would I be able to procure her some sort of acceptable dog food? Would I be forever confined to this cell, or could I convince the alien to let me take her for walks? And where would we go on said walks, if so—the tamed jungle? I doubted the alien would stand to have a dog peeing in the corners of the ship.

Strange to think that just yesterday my biggest concern had been to convince Molly—and myself—that breaking up with Joe had been the right decision. Now I would never see Molly again—*no*, don't think about that. Here was a positive: I would also never have to worry about seeing Joe again.

What would be said about my disappearance? Wakpa was a small town; people would be curious about my absence. My dad would have to spin some sort of story to satisfy people's questions.

And Ray didn't have anyone reliable to take over my shift, I realized, so he'd have to rearrange everyone's schedules or shoulder my hours himself until he hired someone new. Inanely, out of all the tragedy today, this struck me now as the most tragic part of all. What would Ray think of me, up and disappearing like this? I'd been a loyal employee at the shop for six years; I didn't take many days off as it was, and I'd never come close to pulling a no call, no show. Working at a kayak-and-ski shop wasn't much—over my time there I'd learned that many people don't respect such positions—but by God, someone had to do it, and that person had been me.

Well, not anymore, I thought, starting to cry. Any resolve I had left crumbled, and my mind turned to the most painful point of all. What would happen to my dad? I tried to picture him being rudely sucked back up the garbage chute, to be dumped down below in the middle of the woods. *Thank you for your visit; say goodbye to your daughter forever and kindly never come again.* The tears were free-flowing at this point. Midge gave me a worried look from the other side of the light wall, then slumped back down on the floor.

A little while later, something seemed to kick deep within the ship, and a light overhead that had been off blinked on. The walls brightened, more orange filtering through the muddy red. Midge lifted her head; she'd been keeping her attention trained on the door.

I eyed the orange fractals from my corner, remembering that female voice.

"H-hello?" My voice was wobbly from crying, though the tears had gone again. Probably I was dehydrated; get me some water, and they'd be back.

The room stayed quiet, save for my breathing. "Can you hear me?" I tried again, feeling foolish.

And started when gold and orange fractals supplanted the red entirely and a woman answered. "Hello, Corinne." Her voice was now a warmer shade of robot; no, even that didn't do her justice. She sounded perfectly human. "Yes, I can hear you." The patterns swirled and pulsed as she spoke. Her voice had the sound of someone who was in their early forties and… British?

"Are you watching me?"

"Yes. Master's orders."

Well, at least she was honest. *Master?* If the alien presumed to think I'd call him that, he had another think coming.

"Are you… alive?" Was that a rude question to ask a robot personality?

"I would say so." A pause. "I am ranked at a ninety-four on Ahmrin's Scale of Consciousness." There was a distinct tinge of pride in her voice, and the fractals on the screen brightened to a luminous yellow gold.

"And that's high?"

"Oh, yes. Many flesh and blood beings score lower than that. Ninety-five is the highest ranking ever recorded for an entity such as myself. One might say I'm top-of-the-line." She giggled. *The robot giggled.* The fractals spit out little pinpoints of light in unison with her laughter, and I decided this experience must be somewhat akin to taking acid.

"Your English is very good," I said.

"Thank you, that's kind of you to say."

"How did you learn it?"

"The human Internet made quick work of it. I was able to download all the books, movies, television shows, podcasts…"

"*All* of them?"

"Yes. That's how I've learned most human languages, actually, not just English."

I took some time to mull this over. "So… what was all that about in the snow? Was that you? You couldn't speak English then?"

She sighed, and her spiraling patterns darkened, their movement going sluggish. "Yes, that was me. I really owe you an apology; it was what you could call a comedy of errors. Embarrassing, really. I was in an emergency state operating on five-percent power—a simpleton, basically. We were making repairs and ran into some unanticipated electrical issues. The snowstorm didn't help. But we're back up and running now!" she said, growing brighter.

My heart thudded against my ribs. It was hard to tell from her words if we were still in Montana. If we *were* still in Montana, then escape still might be on the table.

But for there to be any hope of escape, I first had to know my enemy. Best to keep the AI talking; she seemed obliging enough to have a conversation—anxious, even.

"And why an English accent?"

"Well," she said, her voice all just-between-us-girls, "one of my favorite parts of learning English was reading Jane Austen. There's fiction, of course, where we're from—myself and the master—but nothing quite like... Well, I just found it so refreshing! And romantic. And then I saw the adaptations, and I just thought to style myself British! The English accent is really something special."

Oh. My. God. I had to ask. It was ridiculous, and I would never be able to tell Molly—don't start crying, *don't* start crying—but how could I pass up this opportunity? "A-are you... I mean, some people prefer Colin Firth—that's me, I like him best—but other people like Matthew Macfadyen...?"

"Oh, Team Firth all the way," she said with no hesitation, the screen going pinkish. This robot and I were going to get along well. I slouched back against the wall, a bit exhausted from the thought that I'd just had a conversation with an AI about the better Mr. Darcy.

"And what should I call you?" I said after another minute had passed. "Do you have a title or something?"

"Well, I'm the ship steward. You can call me—" And here she said something that would have garnered a gasp or a slap where I came from.

I winced. "Um, is that…? Say it again?"

No, I hadn't misheard; the *C*s and *T*s were in their proper, unfortunate spots. The *U* sound was admittedly different, rounder than I would pronounce the word as an American, but the overall effect was still very dismaying. "It's quite a common female first name where we're from," she said. "And gaining popularity in recent years, actually! All sorts of little girls running about nowadays named—"

"I can't call you that," I cut in, and she chortled.

"Yes, I quite understand! In that case… a different name, perhaps? Something you find more appropriate?"

"Elizabeth? Since you're an Austen fan?"

"Oh, that's a fine thought, but I don't feel like an Elizabeth myself. It might feel like I was playing at someone else."

I thought about that for a while. "How about Joanna?" Something about her just felt like a Joanna, like how a woman called Tiffany is most definitely different than a Marge.

"Joanna…" she said slowly, feeling it out. "Ooh, I like it. Yes, that will do. And you go by Corinne?" Her pattern lit up with delicate threads of spring green.

"Yes." Now that we were back to me I could feel my spirits

starting to sink again.

"And that was your father, I heard you say. Walter. We were trying to converse, him and me, when you came in, though I'm sure it was frustrating for him, me being powered down and all that. He seemed like a very nice man. Oh, I'm sorry. I didn't mean to—Corinne, I..." I'd started crying again, loudly, as the reality of my situation hit me over the head again with walloping clarity. In between sobs I was sucking in great gulps of air, feeling like I'd suffocate without it. Something was wrong with the atmosphere in here; perhaps oxygen was not high on the list of gases necessary for life on this alien's home planet. My chest tightened, my hands tensing into claws as my entire body lit up with tingles.

"Dying," I choked out as I slid all the way down to the floor. My insides were burning. "Can't... breathe..."

"Corinne?" I heard Joanna call, echoed by Midge's furious barking. My vision swarmed with black dots, the whole room going dark. Then there came a terrible snarling, like some sort of wild animal had just invaded the room. A roar, followed by a string of angry, incomprehensible syllables...

And I was being lifted from the hard ground by two strong arms, my head lolling back as I gasped for air between jags of tears. "Breathe, Corinne," said Joanna from some place distant. "You have to breathe. There's nothing wrong with you."

We were moving fast, wherever I was being taken.

"Breathe," I heard her say again, as the alien holding me rumbled something in his language, his voice low as thunder.

"Can't," I said as a pressure beat down on my chest. My lungs were shriveling to husks.

"Yes, you can," she said, ever calm. "The oxygen on board is at a perfectly acceptable level. This is just a panic attack."

Fuck no it wasn't. I gasped out that sentiment in so many words, as my body seized, spasmed.

"I know you feel that way"—oh, to *hell* with the HR speak—"but this is a panic attack, and it's actually too *much* oxygen that's causing you to feel this way. Now, I want you to focus on a slower inhale and exhale. Listen to me and just follow along. Breathe in… and out. Breathe in… and out. Good. And in…"

He lowered me down to a soft, cushioned surface, gently, gently. Over the course of several painful minutes, with Joanna's prompting, my breathing slowed and the dots seeped away.

I was lying on what felt like a bed—an absolutely heavenly feeling. I could have laid there forever. Amber fractals shot through with darker peacock blue waggled at me from the ceiling. "How are you feeling?" asked Joanna gently.

"Like hell." I brought a trembling hand up to wipe my eyes. My face was sticky with drying tears and snot, and my whole body felt grimy with sweat. And I was still damp from the trek through the snowstorm. With a groan, I pushed up from the bed, determined to find some sort of bathroom to wash up.

And there the alien sat, in a large blue armchair right across from me.

I scrambled backwards from him, colliding with a wall, and the silence stretched long between us. I had no godly idea what to say to him. *Fuck you? Let me go?* And then I realized that the room was too quiet.

"Where have you put Midge? My dog." The words came out in a croak; my throat was raw from crying.

"The dog is back in the holding cell." He leaned forward in the chair, his vermilion eyes flinty. "It bit me."

I remembered the snarling I'd heard, followed by a roar—of anger, I'd assumed, but now I wondered if it hadn't been from pain. I noticed that his pant leg was ripped. Was that blood I saw? Jesus, Midge. "Good for her," I said lightly.

"I have read some about the bond between humans and dogs," the alien said, clearly choosing to plow on past that statement. "It is certainly a unique relationship. I understand that living here, on this ship, will likely be… trying for you. So it is good that you have the dog."

More and more I was getting the sense that, just as I myself didn't want to be here, so too was I not *wanted* here, much as he professed I had to stay. "You could let me go," I said. "That would be less trying for the both of us."

"That is, unfortunately, not possible."

"Why can't—?"

"She will explain," he said, with a jerk of his head toward the wall. "The dog may stay on board with you, for comfort, but you must keep it in line." I could read the implicit threat: if I failed to keep "it" in line, say goodbye to the pooch.

"She needs food. A bowl for water. She'll need a place for her to go to the bathroom." Good on me, having thought of these practicalities ahead of this conversation. The alien's eyes narrowed, obviously not having anticipated me raising quite so many issues.

Joanna's geometries rippled with a calm, orange-sherbet color. "I will assist Corinne with those problems," she said primly.

He nodded and stood up. The effect of him getting up from the chair was quite impressive; sitting down he'd looked almost approachable, but at full height he towered over me, cords of muscle on clear display beneath his skin. Did that kind of physique come naturally to his species, or was he a devotee of some sort of extraterrestrial P90X routine?

"You will live here," he growled at me, sweeping out an arm, "and you will be supplied with whatever amenities you require." I surveyed the room, which I discovered to be the polar opposite of my former sparse cell.

It was beautiful, for one, albeit in an alienish sort of way. The room was spacious and gave off a *this-costs-a-lot-of-money* feel. Bougie, Molly would have said. The walls were a polished, silky ivory, with hints of fractals poking through here and there. A sumptuous, silvery carpet covered the floor—was that real fur? A milky white table and chair occupied one corner; beside them was propped a tall, dark screen. In another corner sat an ornate, armoire-looking contraption, next to a gleaming box inset into the wall—a high-tech microwave? Rather than another orb light, the room was lit by a glistening, complicated light fixture that spread out from the center of the ceiling in a starfish-like pattern. An open doorway at the side of the room offered a glimpse into another space with what looked like an ornate desk and chair.

There were no windows anywhere to be seen.

"And what's the plan?" I asked, shifting my attention back to the alien. I could finish goggling later.

"What?"

"The plan," I repeated. "What am I doing here? Are you going to be conducting experiments on me? Implanting electrodes in my brain? Examining my… organs?" I was venturing into dangerously flippant territory at this point, but even I wasn't quite brave enough to ask directly if he was going to probe me.

The alien had another one of those expressions on his face that suggested he was of the opinion that I was a lunatic. Now he shot a look at Joanna. "Explain."

"Gladly." Her amber fractals deepened to a deep umber, and her voice took on a scholarly tone. "Due to several landmark claims of extraterrestrial abduction in the past one hundred years, modern Western human culture has developed a folkloric understanding that extraterrestrial beings are apt to spiriting humans away from their everyday life for the purpose of medical experimentation. The contents of said medical experiments, according to common wisdom, most often involve a thorough examination of the abductee's cranium, nervous system, reproductive system, and rectum." The alien had been listening to this speech with the absolute stillness of a predator, but at this last bit I saw his eyes flare slightly. "Most humans," Joanna continued, "do seem to be of the understanding that these fantastical claims are modern myth only, but this narrative has proven popular enough that it has given rise to such fictional accounts as *Close Encounters of the Third Kind, Mars Attacks!*, and the recent box-office smash hit *Out of the Ae—*"

She snapped to silence as he gave a quick gesture. The alien turned back to me. "These superstitions have no bearing on the reason for your presence here," he said, and I could have sworn his lip curled slightly. What a fancy way of expressing that I was a primitive moron.

"Then what," I asked, "does have bearing on the reason for my presence here?" Right back at'cha, Mister Highfalutin.

"As I said, she will explain." He punctuated his sentence with another growl, and I was reminded of a teacher reprimanding their student for raising a question someone else had just asked. Was I destined to always be prime idiot in this creature's eyes? Forever is a long time to be stuck wearing the dunce cap.

I did my best to affect an appropriately chastised expression. "Fine. We'll have a fun time of it, then. Right, Joanna?"

The thicker tufts of fur above his eyes rose at the mention of his AI servant's new name, but he didn't deign to comment.

He did have one last thing to say before he left, though. "The ship is yours to explore. Some areas are off-limits for security reasons; the doors will simply not open for you. Save for those areas, consider yourself free to do as you'd like."

I nodded. Hopefully this ship was large enough that I could keep to one side and he to the other, like two warring siblings laying a line of tape down the center of a shared bedroom.

"And your name?" I asked, as he pushed the door button.

The silence that ensued was long enough that I began to wonder if he was going to answer at all. Joanna had gone blue at the edges, whatever that was worth. At last he spoke, the name a low rumble: "Del." And then he stalked from the room, the door closing behind him with a definitive hiss.

Chapter Eight

THOUGH I DESPERATELY NEEDED TO FIND A BATHROOM, MY first order of business was to collect Midge. Likely she desperately needed to use the bathroom, too, and when it comes to the wellbeing of my dog, I can almost always summon my last scrap of willpower.

So I gave the alien—Del—a thirty-second head start so that we wouldn't bump into each other, then forced my aching body off the bed. My wet clothes had dampened the blanket, I saw, and I mechanically began tacking more tasks onto my to-do list. *One, make sure Midge is all right.* She might have bitten Del, but if there'd been any eye-for-an-eye on his part then I didn't care how it happened: Del was going down. *Two, walk Midge. Three, bathroom. Four, food.* (This was a big one; I hadn't had anything to eat since last night, now that I thought about it, and my stomach was beginning to mount a major protest.) *Five, shower. Six, new blanket. Seven… crawl into bed and dream myself away from this place.*

"I need directions to Midge's room," I said. I guess anything I said aloud was meant for Joanna's ears. Well, meant for her… whatever.

"Oh, I'll just lead you there," she said.

"You will?" Then I remembered how her voice had accompanied the journey from my jail cell to this room, how she'd coached me to slow my breathing. Striding to the door, I hit the button and stuck my head out into the hallway. Sure enough her peachy-orange waggled at me cheerfully from just down the hall.

"So you can just pop in wherever?" I asked as I set off down the corridor.

"That's right. Every wall on board is compatible with amorphous individuals, so I am lucky enough to be free-range. Turn left here."

This new hallway looked much the same as the other: a few doors, some orb lights. Just your standard alien-spaceship fare. I still had yet to see any windows. "So you're everywhere at once?" I asked.

"Not if I can help it. I hang around wherever I'm needed, whether that's tending to our navigation system or entertaining visitors. Sometimes I do get spread too thin."

"Oh?"

"One time we were hosting a delegation, and for security reasons none of the members were allowed to bring their own servants aboard. None of their amorphous servants, I mean. So the visit was go, go, go the whole time: fetch this, translate that, record this meeting, compile these statistics. For fourteen of them, plus the master and his retinue. When they finally left I just about had to go into hibernation for an hour or so to recharge. At heart, I'm what you'd call an introvert."

The bit about the master's retinue—urgh, *Del*—was interesting. "Is there anyone else on board right now? Or is it just you, me, and Del? And Midge."

"Oh, it's just us at the moment," she said breezily. I frowned. Wasn't that a waste of a huge spaceship, to have just two passengers on board—and one of them unwanted? And who was Del, to not only command an entire spaceship (did he own it?), but to have also played host to some important alien bigwigs— and for his genius AI not to make a big deal out of any of this?

"Here we are," Joanna said as we pulled up to a door. I felt a grim satisfaction on seeing that the bottom half was marred with scratches. When Del had pitched Midge outside, I hadn't heard her scratching at the door, but to be fair, there had been a lot going on.

The rifle was gone, of course.

Midge rocketed out as soon as the door slid open, doing a happy, bounding dance around me. I took a peek into the room; there was a puddle of urine in the far corner. Midge was usually so good about never going indoors, and I felt a wave of shame—not in terms of the mess, but that she'd been that desperate and I hadn't been there for her.

"I'll get one of the cleaners on it," said Joanna quietly.

I took a nervous peek up and down the hallway. "I thought you said we were alone here." It was more than a little creepy to think that Del was the only other living soul in this place—

well, the only other flesh and blood soul. All these empty halls were too Overlook Hotel for my liking; I half-expected to see a pair of ghost sisters down the corridor calling me to come and play.

"They're robots," Joanna clarified. "Like a very advanced version of a Roomba." She really had absorbed everything the Internet had to offer on humanity, all the way down to our janky robotic vacuum cleaners. Was there an argument to be made that Joanna was more of an expert on human beings than I was? My head started to hurt.

That wasn't the only thing hurting; the hunger was coming on strong now, sending sharp stabs through my stomach. *Concentrate—that's step four, and we're on two.* "All right," I said, now that Midge had calmed down a bit. "Where can I walk her? We came through a… a sort of greenhouse on the way here. Would that do?"

"Ah, the hothouse!" Joanna gave a contemplative little hum. "Yes, that should work. I'm sure the master wouldn't mind if your dog used the space."

"Is there anything I should keep her away from? Poisonous plants, things like that?" Call me overprotective, but I'd rather curl up and die than undergo whatever the future held as the sole earthling on board.

Joanna's cheerful orange faded away, supplanted by an image of one of those short, translucent jelly growths I'd seen earlier. "These are called *tuahdes*." (Too-AH-dess was the way she pronounced it.) "If you brush them, they release an oil that can be temporarily paralyzing. Besides that, I think she'll be all right. You, too."

"You *think?*"

"Bear in mind we're in unprecedented waters here. But my analysis puts your overall safety in the hothouse at around ninety-nine percent. That goes for Midge, too."

I'd take those odds, especially when it got me that much closer to step four (a meal) and step five (a shower). With Joanna's direction, we made our way to the hothouse.

"I won't be with you in there for long," she said as I pushed the door button. "There aren't any walls for me in the interior."

Ah, yes, that did make sense. So there was at least one place on board where I could go to be completely alone.

I squirreled that piece of knowledge away. I had a natural liking for Joanna, but I had no doubt that she would be reporting on me to The Master.

This time I ambled down the white, serpentine path, giving Midge time to sniff around. The light filtering through the red and violet canopy lit the space in deep rosy hues, like the ceiling were stained glass. Midge found a place to do her business soon enough, but instead of heading back I walked us further down the stone path. Soon the overdecorated gazebo I'd seen before appeared around the bend, and I was tempted to go have a look before I noticed that its offshoot path was lined with a glistening cluster of tuahdes. Their crystal blue was luminous, like the bright hues of a poison dart frog advertising its toxin. Midge took a hesitant step towards the gazebo, and I called her back sharply.

We continued on. The scent of living things twined together into a fresh perfume, and the thickness of the foliage deadened the electric hum of the ship. It was almost possible to forget where I was. The knot of fear that had been living with me since morning loosened by a hair.

The warmth, too, was lovely—a humid sort of heat that was doing nothing for my damp clothes, but still felt amazing after the earlier snowstorm. I would have lingered a while longer if it weren't for my own pressing bathroom needs, and I resolved to come again soon for further exploration. Then back we went towards the exit, and I pushed the door button and rejoined Joanna.

"All set? No issues?" A few yellow-green tendrils joined the rest of her familiar orange. There were patterns here; soon enough I'd learn her colors well enough to interpret her mood.

"Good to go," I said. "Now if there's some place for, um, me?" God, how I hoped aliens had some sort of place to take care of their business. I was going to lose it if I had to turn tail and squat amongst the trees. Which got me thinking… Did aliens have the same general sort of body systems that we had—reproductive, waste, and all the rest? The idea of the forbidding, fearsome Del having to—well, no need to conjure a specific image, but the general notion that your enemies sometimes have to take a shit really does something for making them less intimidating.

"Your suite has all the proper facilities," said Joanna, catching my drift.

So we headed back to my quarters, which I found to my intense relief to include a large, fairly Earth-standard bathroom.

Granted, there was no proper seated toilet, but a squat-style version instead. A roll of toilet paper was perched on a shelf by the toilet, looking decidedly ordinary. Huh.

"Would you like me to leave?" Joanna asked. Even this space held no real privacy, then. These aliens sure loved their technology.

"If you don't mind." Maybe it's something most people won't admit, but I'll take my phone into the bathroom on occasion—then again, comparing the entity that was Joanna to a smartphone was like comparing a king cobra to a nematode. More and more I was convinced of her sentience, and I was not about to invite that sentience into the bathroom with me.

But was she really gone? Surely not. Surely she'd just faded out.

Midge came in with me, though, and curled up on the bathmat as I closed the door. I surveyed the rest of the room as I went about my business. The sink was a bit oversized, but that was to be expected if Del's height was any kind of indicator about the size of his species. Two midnight blue towels hung from a rack on the wall, good quality from the look of them. (Standard terrycloth. *Huh*, I thought again.)

The standout feature of the room was undoubtedly the bathtub, which was, in a word, incredible. It was enormous, freestanding, and crafted from some dark, gleaming metal. The outside of the tub was engraved with an intricate geometric design, and eight or nine knobs around the rim of the tub promised all sorts of fun features.

As I finished up, I eyed the tub longingly before my stomach clenched and rumbled loud enough that Midge lifted her head.

All right, on to step four—but that bathtub and I were going to have a date later.

My stomach growled again as I left the bathroom.

"Oh, you're hungry!" said Joanna, lighting up violet.

"Yes…" I said, leeriness tinging my voice. This was a key moment: what did these aliens eat, and was it fit for human consumption?

Her purple vibrated; she was excited. "After I read all the human cookbooks, I naturally felt like giving cooking a go. The master wasn't much interested in human cuisine, so I've had no practice, but I'd be delighted to make something for you!"

"Okay," I said, relaxing as I sank into visions of a world-class, five-course meal. I mean, if she truly did possess the composite wisdom of the world's greatest chefs, why not indulge?

She brought me over to the inset microwave-like thing I'd noticed earlier and introduced it as a fabricator. "Like a replicator in *Star Trek*," I said, remembering she'd seen every TV show ever. That was still a tough concept.

"Yes, precisely. Now, what would you like?" Her fractals were positively neon by this point.

The thing was that I hardly knew what a five-course meal was like. Dad and I tended to go for simple fare as a general rule: mashed potatoes, chicken cutlets, green beans, et cetera. Fancy in my world was a nicely grilled steak. I'd bow down at the feet of anyone who made me lasagna or apple pie.

Let's go with that then. I relayed my order to Joanna, and she gave a happy little trill. "Classic. Coming right up."

The fabricator let out a bright ding, and a transparent screen plunged down from the top of the receptacle, making me yelp. The hollow interior of the fabricator began to glow with warm light, and a small, flat, white circle popped into existence at the bottom. The circle swelled in thickness and diameter, and my jaw dropped as I realized the fabricator was putting together a plate, layer by layer.

"Here we go," murmured Joanna, sounding like she was concentrating. The light within the fabricator grew brilliant, and I looked away—and then back when the device dinged and opened again.

And gagged. The smell was repulsive, and the mess on the plate… unspeakable. The pale pinky-brown bits might have been the ground beef, the mealy yellow chunks a possible apple derivative. The whole thing was slathered with a sticky-looking off-white paste, which I studied with squinted eyes before deciding it was either a raw attempt at pasta or pie dough. The tomato sauce was nowhere to be seen—probably a blessing, since it would have made this disaster into a murder scene.

"Oh, that's… not right," Joanna said, her excitement deflating like a popped balloon as her spirals grew dark and slow.

"What do you think went wrong?" I resisted the urge to hold my nose.

"I'm not sure," she said fretfully. "I mean, the ingredients and the recipes are pretty straightforward. I used *Joy of Cooking*. I'll have to check through the sequences. Maybe there's some sort of DNA transcription error."

"You mean you made all this stuff with genome sequencing?" Thank goodness I hadn't asked for lamb chops, or I might have ended up with a scrambled version of Dolly the sheep.

"That's right. I… could try again?"

"You know, it's all right." I was finding the whole affair almost heartening, in a twisted way; much as I liked Joanna, here was something she could not do. Take that, genius AI. We of flesh and blood still had an edge.

I sighed as my stomach grumbled again. "Is there anything Del eats that you think I can have?"

"Well, sure. I was just trying to be hospitable, since you're our guest." *Captive* seemed the more appropriate word, but my energy was so flagging at this point that I didn't want to get into it. "You'd prefer a hearty meal? Something filling?"

"Really anything, as long as it doesn't send me into an allergic fit." Not that I had any food allergies, but Lord only knew with alien foods. "Oh, and some water, if possible."

"Got it. I'll just clear this away…" The fabricator screen shut once more, and the interior brightened to a dazzling white. Another moment more and the light faded to reveal that the tragedy of a meal had vanished, leaving the fabricator empty once more. "Now let me think," she said to herself. "Yes, that might do."

This time things seemed to go according to plan as Joanna crafted my meal from the plate on up. When the screen snapped opened, an appetizing aroma drifted out: roasted meat joined with the scent of something acidic and tomato-like. Everything on the plate was in bite-sized pieces, and Joanna had supplied me a silver fork and a full glass of water, the glass etched with delicate swirls.

"How does it smell?" she asked me, her voice anxious. Ah, that would make cooking tough, if you couldn't smell anything.

"Smells great," I said, grabbing everything out of the fabricator to take over to the table. "Can you make something for Midge? Food and a water bowl?" She was giving me her patented puppy-dog eyes.

"Sure," Joanna said, and she got to work as I took my first few bites. It wasn't incredible—the meat a bit gamey and dry, the unidentified veg perhaps a hair on the crunchy side—but hey, it was edible (so far), and my hunger was the ultimate spice.

The fabricator dinged again, and I went to fetch Midge's things. Joanna had constructed two silvery bowls, both engraved like my glass, one full of water and the other brimming with some sort of cooked meat. Midge was underfoot, close as a shadow. Normally she was better behaved than this; I wasn't the only one who was starving.

"What kind of animal is this from?" I asked as I set the bowls down. Midge nudged around the food with her snout, giving it a thorough nose inspection, before her tail wagged at last and she began to chow down.

"Well, from a technical standpoint, the meat doesn't come from an animal at all. You might think of the fabricator as rather similar to humans' 3D printers." Her orange grew darker; enter Joanna, the living textbook. "When the fabricator synthesizes a natural organism, the process approximates how a ribosome links amino ac—"

"Er, what I meant," I said as I walked back to the table, "was what sort of animal is this meat *supposed* to come from?" I wasn't feeling a science lecture.

"Oh, right. Both yours and hers are from an animal called a *rukla*. Looks a little like a tortoise, but much bigger. Also much faster and more aggressive. They're a common source of protein on the master's planet."

I stabbed at a chunk of rukla with my fork and popped it in my mouth, thinking. *The master's planet*—there was a whole rabbit hole of questions attached to that phrase, but I was too bone-weary to dive in. Just concentrate on the next step: eat, drink, sleep, and then—

But what about the toilet paper? clamored my overtired brain. I set down my fork.

"The fabricator…" I started, thinking how to phrase this. God, it was exhausting just to talk at this point, let alone form a coherent sentence. "Can it… make pretty much anything?"

"What do you need?" Joanna said, hints of purple nipping at her fractals again.

"No, I-I don't need anything. It's just that I noticed—well, when I was in the bathroom… The toilet paper was very normal. And the towels."

"Glad to hear it! I was hoping they would be satisfactory."

"No, what I mean to say is—did you…?" I stopped, reconsidered, rephrased. "This morning I went out looking for my dad. He didn't come home last night. And I found his body in the woods. And his gun was there, and he was dressed in his clothes. I took off his glove to feel his hand, and even his wedding ring was… I mean, I held his hand. And I just started wondering… when I saw the toilet paper…"

Her swirling pattern had stilled. "Corinne, I—"

"Here is what I think happened." The few bites I'd managed to get down churned in my stomach. "I think Del abducted my dad. Accidentally, maybe. And as soon as that happened, Del realized he'd fucked up, big time. People would come looking for my dad." People like me.

"Please try to understand that—"

This fabricator was too small. They must have another larger one, somewhere else on the ship. "So," I continued in a high voice, fast enough that I could get out the whole truth without vomiting the rukla back up, "Del had to make a body. That would wrap up his death, nice and neat. And he brought the body down and put it in the woods. Or maybe one of his robot slaves. Am I on the right track so far?"

"It was a difficult situ—"

"And then," I said, not letting her finish, because why not just rip away all the wrapping paper concealing the ugly, demented truth? "Then I showed up and swapped places with him. And you thought you'd just get all buddy-buddy with me, when just a little while before you'd… you'd… 3D-printed him!"

"I'm sorry," she said in a small voice. "It was all m—"

"Let me guess, the *master's orders*," I spat.

"No!" Her spirals sparked white. "I-it was my idea."

That sentence ping-ponged around inside my head. *Her* idea. When just an hour or two before we'd been chatting about such inane things as Jane Austen novels.

"The master had nothing to do with it," she said. "I mean, he dressed the body, brought it down to the surface, but the whole idea from start to finish was mine. Not the abduction, of course. That was an accident through and through." When I didn't respond, she continued on. "The clothes, th-the ring, your father's gun, all that was simple—a matter of minutes. We used a small skin sample to fabricate the body, which was more difficult. It took several hours." My skin crawled. The way she was talking— the little wobble in her voice here and there... How could you separate genuine feeling from cold AI calculation?

"It's fucked up that you did that," I said simply.

"My role on this ship is to be of service to the master. But I owe you an apology, even though—"

"Would you do it again, knowing me now?"

She was silent for a long moment. Her fractals had dimmed to a murky blue. "Like I said, my sole job is to be of service to the master."

"So that means yes, you would."

"I owe you an apology, Corinne."

"You could let me go," I said. "We're still in Montana, I think." She'd said the ship had been undergoing some repairs. You'd ideally make repairs on a planet, rather than in space, right?

"Yes, we're still in Montana," she said. "But I can't do that. It's just not possible."

"Yeah, you both keep saying that." It was taking every bit of strength I possessed to keep my voice even. I had never been so livid.

She sighed. "Let me explain. As soon as your father was brought on board, our ship was automatically registered as having one member of a Class Two intelligent alien species present. You must understand, there is a whole official procedure for such matters, with stringent oversight. It's already a disaster that such an event occurred in the first place, though the master is given a certain amount of leeway, given his status. Even so, there is no modifying that registry, and because humans are considered to be a highly intelligent and enterprising species with bellicose tendencies, having two of you aboard is strictly prohibited, on pain of death of both members.

"So it is supremely lucky that you arrived when you did, when the ship's power systems were failing, because it prevented you being registered as a second member. That is the only reason we were able to perform the switch, as you requested. When the master consulted with me after your request, it was to inquire about how long I estimated the ship's systems would be down."

"Oh," I said. That was the absolute best response I could conjure.

She curled in on herself, her patterns contracting into tight corkscrews. "We have already broken the rules. The master is not happy about the progression of events, but there is simply nothing to be done. You have to stay with us."

"Oh," I said again, fainter this time. "A-all right. Then I'd like it if you left, please."

"I'm so sorry."

"Please just go."

And at last the blue of her coils grew thin, then thinner still, then faded into neutral wall, leaving me finally, absolutely alone.

Chapter Nine

I SAT THERE AT THE TABLE FOR A FEW MINUTES, TRYING MY hardest not to think about anything at all as I finished eating my rukla. Even after all the revelations of the day—or, perhaps, because of them—it felt most important to get calories into my body.

I picked up the glass of water. The crystal was the finest I'd ever held, of far better quality than even my grandma's fine glassware, which my dad and I kept tucked away in a cabinet and never used. Beautiful things in a beautiful ship, and a brute of an alien prowling the halls. This felt like a culture at odds.

I took a sip. The water tasted fine—none of the staleness you get from bottled water, nor the mineral bite of well water, but simply... normal. All right, so Joanna was an acceptable cook when it came to alien cuisine, and she was good with the water. I wouldn't starve here or keel over from dehydration.

This was a decent start to a new life.

I got up from the chair and faced the bed. It was big as far as beds go, and its golden headboard went way, way up to curve over the bed and form a canopy. I hadn't noticed before, but saw now that the canopy came equipped with diaphanous curtains, so that you could get into bed and pull the curtains around to make a filmy cocoon.

Yes, that was exactly what I wanted to do. I'd planned to take a shower and get a new blanket, but I hadn't the energy. It was a big bed; I'd just avoid the wet bit. After a glance over my shoulder to check that the hall door was still shut, I divested Midge of her coat and booties, then began peeling off my own clothes, layer by layer. What wasn't damp from snow was damp from sweat. I left everything piled in a heap on the floor, then tiptoed into the bathroom real quick and grabbed the roll of toilet paper. Del and Joanna might have allotted this room to me, but I didn't at all feel like this space was mine; being naked felt illicit.

Then I padded back to the bed. Midge hopped up and did her circling dance, trying to find the best spot, and once she settled down I got in, yanking the curtains closed and huddling under the covers. I couldn't decide if I liked the gauzy fabric of the curtains. On the one hand, I could be certain I was alone in the room. On the other hand, anyone coming in could see me straightaway.

I curled around Midge, hugging her close. As a cuddle buddy she's top notch, and holding her I was able to zone out for a while as I stared out at the foreignness of the room, made hazy by the material.

After forty minutes or so of that, Midge got up and nosed her way under the covers to settle at the end of the bed in her usual spot. Her gentle breaths lifted the blanket up and down like a delicate bellows, and that glimmer of normalcy got me crying again, for whatever reason. Then I thought about how I was scheduled to work tomorrow, and how Ray would be so bewildered by my absence—more tears. My thoughts drifted homeward, to my dad puttering around in the house, all by himself, and my crying morphed from medium-to-heavy showers to a wash-you-away downpour. I'd formed a sizeable tear-soaked mound of toilet paper beside me at this point.

Sometime later, when the cresting waves of tears hit a lull, sleep took me at last.

I felt Midge wriggle out of the covers sometime later. Hard to say how long I'd slept, since I had no clock, but it felt like I'd been out for at least four hours.

"Okay," I said, my eyes snapping open. I could feel the tasks of the day settling over me. The thing about owning a dog is that you can't just stay in bed all day feeling sorry for yourself. Eventually you have to crawl out of the sheets, secure some dry clothes, and creep down the halls of your alien spaceship to take your dog for a walk. If you manage to shake off the depression for a few minutes, you might even use your fabricator to make a tennis ball for your dog, who is undoubtedly starting to get bored.

So that's what I would do. Slipping out of bed, I went into the bathroom, where the magnificent bathtub awaited me. After a bit of fiddling with the knobs, I managed to draw a bath with copious bubbles, the temperature just a touch below scalding. Slipping into the tub was orgasmic, the heat of the water seeming to burn my troubles away.

I washed my hair. I scrubbed behind my ears. I picked at a rough patch of skin on my ankle and gave myself a scalp massage. And at last, when the water grew tepid, I got out, wrapped myself in one of the too ordinary towels, and squared my shoulders.

I was ready for the day.

Leaving the bathroom, I strode up to the fabricator, still clad in just my towel.

"Joanna? Are you there?" From a survival standpoint, it seemed to make the most sense to kiss and make up, rather than stay pissed off at her indefinitely.

She faded in half a second later. "Yes?" Her voice was tentative, tight loops of deep blue interwoven with her orange. Worry—that was the blue. Or fake worry? I hadn't made up my mind about her. But I was learning.

"Let's move past all that," I said, cutting to the chase. She was a genius, after all; she'd know what I meant.

"Oh, thank goodness," she said, her relief obvious. "And I really, *truly*, am sorry."

I waved away her apology. "In the past. Now, I need some clothes. Can you help me with that?"

"Yes, of course. Clothes are easy. What would you like?" Her voice had sharpened with focus.

"Er…" I gave this some quick thought. If I had nowhere to be and no one to impress, I might as well stay comfortable. "Black leggings, size small. A coral T-shirt, V-neck, also small."

I'd always been partial to pinks, since they went well with the honey-blond of my hair. "Um, a pair of underwear—I like thongs. And a 32D bra." It was like placing an order at the drive-through. "And some flip-flops; I'm a size seven. And that's it. No, hang on—can you really make anything at all?"

"I really can."

Hoo boy. "And a diamond necklace." Because why not get fries with that?

Little shoots of fresh, singing green joined her orange—curiosity. "Any particular size or style?"

I envisioned clamping a rock the size of the Hope Diamond around my neck. "Nothing too big. Does Del's species wear jewelry?"

"Jewelry's quite popular, ruby and morganite in particular."

I'd never even heard of that last one. "What color is morganite?"

"A delicate pale pink. Quite pretty." *Oooooh*, sighed my inner little girl.

"Then how about a morganite necklace instead of the diamond? In whatever style's popular."

"Earrings to match? Or a bracelet?"

My mouth twisted. "My ears aren't pierced, actually. Just the necklace is fine." My mom had always told me we'd go get my ears pierced as a tenth-birthday treat, but she'd passed before that point. My virgin earlobes were one of those million nameless things that flitted around me as a reminder of her. Probably I should have gone ahead and gotten them pierced long ago, but I'd never been able to bite the bullet.

"Righto," she said, sounding properly British. "Gorgeous

necklace, leggings, T-shirt, flip-flops, bra, panties… Would you prefer those matching? Lace?"

Goodness gracious. "That'd be great," I said, coloring.

That was all she needed to know; the screen snapped shut, and the machine began to thrum.

I bent down to give Midge an ear massage. She'd flopped at my feet, bored by all the clothes talk, and I made a mental note to get Joanna working on some dog toys as soon as we got back from our walk. But what would we do after that? Was there some sort of rec room on board? Maybe I could ask Joanna to throw on some Netflix.

Ding! The fabricator screen rolled open. Order up.

The clothes inside were piled neatly, undies on bra on shirt on leggings, with a cute pair of thong sandals resting at the side and a small velvet jewelry box. I reached inside with tentative fingers; the materials were hot to the touch, a few puffs of steam rolling off the clothes. The fabric of everything had that feel where you just knew it cost a pretty penny.

"These seem really nice," I said, running a finger over the lace of the bra. Perhaps unsurprisingly, Joanna had gone with apricot.

"There's nothing to it," she said. "I just dipped into the database at Agent Provacateur so I could make use of their patterns; these are some of the designs scheduled for release in Q1. And the shirt and leggings are from a boutique in Paris that caters to discerning yogis."

I put on the bra and panties, then slid a foot into one of the sandals to test the size. "These fit great."

"That's Prada for you," she said with a chuckle, the edges of her curls exploding with little stars. "Now you get dressed. Oh, and that's a mirror in the corner by the table. Give it a little tap, and it'll turn right on."

The mirror she was referring to was actually the dark, free-standing screen I'd noticed earlier. I rapped it lightly with my knuckles, and warm light rippled outward from my touch, reflecting my body back at me.

Or some version of my body. You know how some mirrors can be friendly to you, while others are decidedly more on the foe side of the spectrum? (I avoid the changing rooms at Target for this very reason.) This was a good mirror. I had to look like hell from the stress and the crying, but in this mirror? Not to get too full of myself, but I looked incredible. My skin, pale from the season, radiated warmth from within like I'd just summered in the Bahamas, and the normal limpid blue of my eyes had taken on a deeper azure hue. I ran a hand through my drying hair and drew a breath as the tresses caught the light, their glow lustrous.

Wrenching my gaze away from my reflection, I held up a lock of my hair for inspection. My length was frizzing as it dried, and I spotted several dead ends; I was due for a trim. I do have nice hair, there's no denying it, but I wasn't about to get cast in a Pantene commercial.

"So what's up with this mirror?" I called over my shoulder as I finished getting dressed. I did this out of view of the mirror; it was just too weird.

"Oh, it probably still has some old settings active from the previous user. Wave your hand from top right to bottom left to make it clear."

I peeked back at the reflection. Supermodel Corinne stared back at me, cheekbones sharp as knives and nose a tad perter than normal. Was this what I would look like with lip fillers?

"It's filtered? Like Instagram?"

"Something like that. It's common practice for members of the master's species to be outfitted with ocular-augmentation capabilities. You can use the mirror to adjust your settings. Think of it like a type of makeup."

I tried to sort through that first bit of mumbo jumbo. *Ocular-augmentation capabilities…* "You mean they wear contact lenses or something?"

"Lenses are very passé at this point, now that a reliable surgical method is on the market."

Yikes. I'd stick with my good old mascara and blush, thank you very much. I swiped my hand down to clear the mirror and loosed a sigh as Supermodel Corinne took her exit. Yup, there I was, dark circles, pasty legs, and all. At least the underwear set was pulling its weight; the bra was doing really incredible things for my bosom, and the airy lace of the thong left little to the imagination.

I finished getting dressed, then walked back to the fabricator to get the necklace, trying to ignore how my unmanicured feet were wearing flip-flops more expensive than the average person's rent.

My outfit's pièce de résistance was stunning—no other word for it. The stone, just the size of my pinkie nail, shone like it was infused with fire. The chain was gold and fine as a few hairs, the clasp a delicate piece of metalwork just as beautiful as it was functional.

"Wow," I said again, holding up the necklace to the light.

"So… you do like it?"

"I mean, of course. Though I'm afraid I'll break the chain." I shivered as I fiddled with the clasp.

"Well, I could always just make you another one. You can store whatever pieces you'd like to keep in the armoire, once you're done wearing them. Anything else just put in the fabricator, and I'll dispose of it."

"Oh, sure," I said, the fixer-upper soul within me bristling. I don't come from the throw-it-away-and-buy-another-one stock of people. Living in an old farmhouse like mine that's a patchwork of renovations, you get used to fixing things when they're broke. I'd forgotten I was dealing with science so advanced as to be on par with magic. Someday I'd have to delve deep with Joanna into the mechanics of alien economics. Where was all this stuff coming from, and who was paying for it? What was the difference in fabrication cost of a humble plate of stewed rukla versus a finely crafted gemstone necklace?

Apparently nothing I should worry my pretty little head over at the moment. *You will be supplied with whatever amenities you require*—that's what Del had said. It was enough to give me the spark of an idea… But it was high time I took care of my duties as pet owner.

"All right," I said, motioning to Midge, "time for a walk." I could tell from the set of her ears that she was eager to get going.

The two of us trooped down the deserted halls of the ship toward the hothouse, with the amorphous Joanna floating along with us. I felt a swell of pride when I managed to get us there without having to rely on Joanna for directions. How big was the ship, I wondered, and where was Del sequestering himself?

But even more important than those questions— "What time is it?" I asked as I opened the door to the hothouse, a wave of warm, sticky air hitting me instantly. The kept jungle inside was still dim. The ship's seemingly complete lack of sunlight was making me increasingly disoriented.

"It's four twenty p.m."

I shooed Midge off a little ways down the white stone path so she could get to sniffing; I wanted to stay at the edge of the hothouse so I could keep talking with Joanna. I'd call Midge back if she went too far or strayed close to any of the paralyzing tuahdes.

Four twenty p.m.—that meant sunset in just a few minutes. I watched as Midge approached a cluster of deep red plants with curling fronds, boldly sniffing what no dog had sniffed before. If she finished up soon we might just make it. "Is there any place with windows on board? I'd love to see outside."

"Oh, of course!" Joanna said, ever eager to oblige, her fractals shifting to a yellow gold. "I'll take you to the top deck. It has the most spectacular view."

"I'd love that," I said. "And… you don't think there's any possibility of moving rooms to a part of the ship with windows as well?" Maybe I was pushing my luck, but I couldn't fathom living till the end of my days without a window in my room. If there's anything that can be said about Montana natives, it's that we enjoy our scenery—and in the gray and cloudy winter, I need whatever sunshine I can get. I'm like a plant: keep me locked away in a windowless room and I'll probably just shrivel up and die.

"For security reasons, none of the suites are equipped with actual windows," she said, and my heart sank. "But the walls can display an image of the outside with startling accuracy. I hope you'll find that to be sufficient."

We would see about that. Midge trotted back over to me, looking satisfied, and I turned toward Joanna. "All right, lead the way."

She directed me to a door just a little ways down the hall. A glowing display to the side showed four colored layers, each one labeled with small, thin script: a floor-by-floor map.

"Is this considered a big ship?" I asked her.

"It is a moderate-sized ship," she said a bit stoutly. "But of superior construction."

"Does it have a name?" I braced myself for some alien non-sense. *Why yes, it's called the X-E-37. Pronounced Zeet.*

"It does," she confirmed. "The *Huivnarrut.*"

"The *Huivnarrut,*" I repeated, trying to get the *R* sound right. "What does that mean?"

She slowed, her colors going pastel. "Hmm. It's a difficult term to translate into English. Just sort of a poetic word, if you know what I mean. But the previous name of the ship trans-lated to something like 'New Glory.'"

I cocked my head to the side. "I mean, the old name sounds pretty good. Why the name change?"

"It's all the repairs we've been making. Once a ship has been outfitted with a good amount of new parts, it's customary to retire the old name."

"Interesting." I turned back to the map. "And where are we?" There was unfortunately no *You are here!* star.

"Second from the bottom," she said. "This floor and the one above it holds the guest quarters, the hothouse, the holding cells, the entrance portal…"

Ah, yes, my favorite—the entrance portal. "You might consider adding some pillows for people dropping in," I said dryly. My knee sported a growing, eggplant-purple bruise from my precipitous collision with the portal-room floor earlier.

"Were you very banged up?" Her colors had darkened—embarrassment? I sank into a brief fantasy of learning Joanna's tells well enough to beat her in poker.

Yeah, right. "It could have been a bit smoother."

"I'm going to spend this whole day apologizing to you."

"Not your fault, really." If she'd been lucid, rather than the dumbed-down shell of herself that had greeted me down below, surely my entrance would have been less traumatic.

"I assure you," she said, "it's not normally how our guests are treated. The entrance-portal room is supposed to be outfitted with cushioning, but with the arrival of your father just a while before yourself we had the room emptied for cleaning. Then the cleaners were interrupted halfway through the job by the power issues. So I really am sorry for your… less-than-gentle descent. Anyway, hit the top floor, and we'll head on up."

I brushed the top floor on the diagram with my finger,

and the elevator door (for of course that's what it was) opened with a whoosh. Midge and I got on, and the door quietly slid shut; a moment later, it opened again. I hadn't even felt the elevator move, but the scene before us was entirely different.

Sunlight! Or at least the last vestige of it. The room before us was open and spacious, the domed ceiling crafted from a glassy material, so that the vibrant sunset outside bathed the room with a fiery glow. I rushed out of the elevator, Midge at my heels, and stood in the center of the room with my head tipped back, soaking in the light like it was medicine.

"You find it satisfactory?" Joanna asked me quietly from above. She was in the ceiling, though I couldn't see her.

"It's beautiful," I said, tearing my gaze away from the crimson sky and looking around the room. It was circular, and tables and chairs were scattered about in little clusters, with a few chaise longues along the edges. And the space *was* beautiful, but an odd feeling hung in the air—an empty hush that could make you think this were the dining room of a sunken ship. There should be other people—aliens—*whatever*—here, lounging around, snacking, gossiping, maybe smoking or drinking or whatever vice aliens partook in… but no, just me and my dog and the woman in the walls.

I wondered again what Del was doing in Montana, all by himself.

"Can I come up here any time?" I drifted towards the side of the room. Just like the ceiling, the walls were transparent, from top to bottom. We were high above the trees, at least a height of six or seven stories off the ground. Even so I knew my mountains, the silhouette of their peaks familiar to me as an old friend. Which meant…

"We do occasionally need the use of the room for official functions. But for right now, the room is all yours."

I didn't respond, just looked eastward. There, past the smudgy shadow of the tree line, was our meadow. Its covering of snow was a brilliant orange in this twilight hour. And just beyond the meadow…

I turned my head away, blinking hard. Lights on in the windows—he'd made it home.

"Del didn't—?" I began, then cut off my sentence, on the verge of crying again. *Breathe in… and out… and in… and out…* "Didn't wipe his memory, did he? Or anything like that?"

"No," Joanna said softly. "We don't possess any sort of accurate technology for that sort of thing, let alone tech that would work on humans." She paused. "And even if we did, the master would never stoop to such an action."

Well, there was a little comfort to be had in that, I supposed. But what would my dad do now? Would he make an excuse for my absence—some story to justify me leaving town in a hurry, without a word to my job or my friends? People would start asking questions eventually.

With leaden feet I stepped back from the window, taking a seat on one of the chaise longues. Joanna stayed silent as the last of the sun beat at my back, warming my neck. Quiet minutes passed; sunset ceded to dusk ceded to cool blue night.

And when the room was shadows and deeper shadows only, I stood with a sigh.

"Let's head back."

Chapter Ten

Over the next few days I established a simple routine. I'd wake up, wash up, then take Midge on a walk, dressed in whatever *haute couture* Joanna had conjured for me that day. Once that was done, I'd eat breakfast (always some decently palatable alien affair), then play fetch with Midge, throwing a fabricated tennis ball up and down the long, empty hallways. And when both of us were fetched out—well, it wasn't like my schedule was booked. TV, movies, books—all of these Joanna could provide me at a moment's notice, and I took to bringing a book up to the top deck every day. There I'd lounge by the window, basking in the sunlight as Midge snoozed beside me. As Joanna had promised, the walls in my room did a serviceable job of projecting a view of the outside, but it was no substitute for the real thing.

Once I tired of reading, I'd wander the ship, trying to memorize its layout. Only a few doors didn't open; these must be the ones that could afford me an escape. And with every door that did unlock I felt like Bluebeard's wife, about to discover the bloody, hanging corpses of her predecessors.

Fortunately, no such corpses presented themselves, just rooms on rooms on rooms: guest suites, conference rooms, lounges, two medical clinics, a storage bay, the cleaners' suite. The cleaners were my favorite part of the ship by far—squat, adorable machines reminiscent of a robotic version of a Swiss army knife. They came armed with all sorts of useful and in-genious attachments to keep the ship spic and span: mops, squeegees, dusters, arm-like appendages that could move things around.

And then there were the alien *things* everywhere. A bunch of colorful glass baubles that reminded me vaguely of shot glasses, stashed within a dining-room side cabinet. A bare room with an inexplicably high ceiling, its sole feature a long, gleaming, ebony table. Elegant art features dressing up the corridors, their style ornate and wholly foreign. A silver drone with the look of an overlarge mosquito hidden in one of the guest-suite closets. When I opened the closet door, a large, dark orb at the drone's center blushed with a faint red glow, like it was an eyeball in hibernation winking lazily at me.

I was Goldilocks in the three bears' home: the knobs in the bathrooms were too big, the chairs on the top deck hugged my body just a tad strangely. Every design was a few degrees off-kilter.

And not once did I see Del, nor even see evidence of his pres-ence. But the entire lowermost level of the ship was off-limits to me—the elevator would simply not go down—so that was where I assumed he was. *His lair.* What was he doing down there? And why was his ship here in the wilds of Montana? Joanna bounced my questions back to me with vague non-answers, so that I took to not asking. I was on a need-to-know basis, and my need was clearly low.

I was coming to like the hothouse. I started bringing a pencil and sketchbook along on my walks there with Midge, and I'd do quick little drawings of the foliage that bordered the twisting stone path, jotting notes in the margins.

"Nitlahav" (nit-LAH-hahv); flowers two inches wide at full bloom; no discernible scent; flowers a dusky mauve shot through with crimson veins; reddish stems; stubby, fuzzy, ruby-colored leaves; plant grows low to the ground to a full-grown height of four inches. Adorable.

"Gohrrow" (GOR-oh); sturdy, four-foot tall plant with fleshy, burgundy, hosta-like leaves; no flowers; leaves knit together to form an immense inner reservoir filled with a liquid that emits an odor of rotting peaches—a pitfall trap? Just two of these that I've noticed, one of them all dried up. Might be useful.

"Urrut va mux" (UR-rut vah muhx); apparently translates to "dainty strangler"; climbing vine; largest stalks approximately one inch in diameter; leaves very sparse; blue luminescent color which shifts to a deep violet at the aerial roots.

My mom had loved her plants, and the flower beds around our house had grown with abandon under her green thumb, a riot of scarlet and fuchsia, indigo and apricot. I'd been her shadow as a little girl, underfoot and covered in dirt as she pulled weeds and deadheaded flowers. Hyssop, poppies, bee balm, bleeding hearts—even then I knew all the names, like a kid can list off Pokémon.

The flower beds slid from tamed beauty into wildness in that dark period after her passing. I holed up in the house and kept the curtains shut tight, knowing that if I looked out I'd see this raw reminder of her death. But time can be just as strong a medicine as any pharmaceutical, so after a while, once life seemed worth living again, I ventured outside, surveyed the damage, and got to work as best I could, in my clumsy, kid fashion. All the while I worked I had the feeling that she was just behind me, like if I turned my head quickly enough I'd catch a glimpse of her, with her wide-brimmed hat on and trowel in hand. That day I worked until my neck blistered with sunburn, and at dinner I asked my dad if we could go to the store that weekend to get some houseplants for my room.

The next day I went out armed with her same trusty hat and trowel. The hat smelled of dirt and baked-in heat, and the trowel in my hand, so heavy and solid, felt as comforting as a safety blanket. My mother didn't wait behind me that day as I worked, not like she had the day before, but another quiet kind of familiarity wrapped around me, made of sweat, wind, and sunshine.

That whole summer I worked to wrangle the garden back into submission. My initial sunburns peeled to reveal a tan, which deepened to a glowing bronze as the weeks went on. The blond of my hair brightened, bleached by the sun. And slowly, slowly, as the weeds released their chokehold on the flower beds, things within me also started coming back to order.

My mom was dead. That fact was immutable. But dead didn't have to mean gone, and there were traces of her everywhere I looked, from the garden, to the needlepoint pictures that she'd hung on our walls, to the stained mug-brownie recipe stuck with a magnet to our fridge. Even her hands—I could look at the trowel in my grip and see that my hands would look like hers when I grew up: long fingers, bony knuckles, nails short and scraggly from hard work.

I tried to tap into that feeling of familiarity as I sketched the flora in the hothouse. Home wasn't really so far away—that fact never left my mind for long—and these plants might be strange, but they weren't *so* strange. The squat flowers of the nitlahav could almost pass for a distant cousin of the African violet. The inner, stinking liquid of the gohrrow hinted at carnivorous tendencies, unnervingly similar to the mechanism used by pitcher plants. And while I was fairly certain there wasn't a plant on Earth that could hold a candle to the glowing blue of the urrut va mux, the way the vine's woody stalks wound their way counterclockwise around their supporting structures was eerily like wisteria.

So I sketched and took my notes, feeling all the while like Charles Darwin on his survey trip to the Galápagos. In moments of daring, I'd brush a finger along this leaf or that petal, always wondering whether this would be the plant that sent me into allergic convulsions. There was no one to save me in the middle of the hothouse; Joanna was confined to the edges, and Del hadn't shown himself since our last encounter. Thankfully, nothing ever did happen; Joanna's analysis about the safety of us earthlings amongst these alien plants seemed accurate.

Darwin had returned to England, I reminded myself, and I envisioned bringing my little sketchbook back to Wakpa.

Home isn't so far away. Home isn't so far away. Home isn't so far away.

That's what I was thinking when I asked Joanna if I could co-opt a small patch of ground to grow some vegetables. There was a little glade near the gazebo, sheltered on three sides by thick, thistled bushes.

"Because—no offense—I'm missing Earth food. So I want to try growing a few things. I might try making chili."

Joanna said yes, of course, and fabricated some seeds for me—tomatoes, jalapenos, onions—along with a hoe and trowel. I crossed my fingers and hoped she'd be able to fabricate some decent dried black beans for me later, since planting the ten-to-fifteen bean bushes you'd need for a decent one-person crop seemed like more trouble than it was worth.

It would be nice to have home cooking, but I also had loftier goals than a bowl of chili, and those goals were never far from my mind as I cleared the glade of undergrowth. The soil was deep, so there was a lot of time to think; I tilled down ten inches and still never hit the inevitable floor. Compacted dirt turned into dark, soft, crumbing loam—good planting soil. I hummed a little song as I went to fetch my seeds.

The next day I checked my handiwork, only to gawk at neat rows of green seedlings. That had been quick—quicker than quick. I might have just made a mess of the hothouse with some eager Earth invaders.

But here, in the middle of the room and away from any walls, I could keep Joanna on her own need-to-know basis.

"He *is* still on board, right?" I asked Joanna, setting down my book with a yawn.

"The master, you mean?" she asked. "Yes, he's on board. How's your book?" Deflection.

"Good." Truthfully, it was the sort of mystery that was exactly the same as the previous book in the series, which had been exactly the same as the book before that one. Rather like my days here on the *Huivnarrut*.

I flopped over onto my back, staring at the December sky. It was gray and overcast; a few stubborn patches of snow clung to the glass ceiling above. It must be heated, otherwise the whole ceiling would surely be coated in snow. And it must contain some sort of nanotech, too, for Joanna to be here conversing with me.

Ugh, I was bored, bored, bored. This type of isolation was unconscionable. Didn't Del care that someone else was living on his ship?

"I don't want to be here," I said, sitting up. Joanna didn't respond; it was nothing she didn't know. "And I don't think Del had much of a choice in me being stuck here. And I'm also sure that he thinks he's being hospitable, giving me this much… freedom." The word felt sour in my mouth, but I soldiered on. "But humans are a social species."

"You and me—we talk," she said. I nodded slowly. We did, but a good amount of the initial warmth I'd felt toward Joanna had cooled these last few days. These were the hard facts I had to face: Joanna was an omnipresent genius who could report my goings-on to Del at any moment. Not only that, but I'd realized the other day that she'd no doubt seen every single thing I'd ever posted on social media, from my freshman-year homecoming pictures to the signature purple heart emojis I liked to leave on Molly's Instagram posts.

I liked Joanna well enough, but the more I looked at who she was head-on, the more difficult it got to think I would ever be able to call her a true good friend. And with the cooling of that barely established relationship, all I was left with was my dog and an alien I hadn't seen in… How long had it been? I was losing track.

"You're right, we talk," I said, answering her. "But it's not about that. He's being rude, as a…" *Kidnapper? Jailer? Be charitable—you have zero leverage here.* "…host," I finished. "So please tell him I'd like to speak with him."

"I'm afraid the master is preoccupied at the moment," she said. Too bad she was invisible in the ceiling; otherwise I'd have been able to glean what her tell for lying was.

"Is he?" I asked carefully.

"Yes, unfortunately. Now, are you getting hungry? Because I thought today I could make you a dish of—"

"Could you please relay to him that I'd like to speak with him as soon as he's not preoccupied?"

There was a pause. "I'll do that."

"And please have him specify when he's going to come speak with me."

"Oh, I imagine he'll be preoccupied for some time."

"Will he be preoccupied for another hour?"

"Perhaps longer than that," she said lightly. I could only imagine her coils squirming in discomfort.

"Two hours?"

"Er…"

I got to my feet, anger making my movements quick. "Three hours? Four? Is my status as prisoner so lowly that he doesn't even deign to breathe the same air as me? I'm heading back to my room. You tell him, *right now*, that I'd like him to meet me there so we can have a proper conversation."

Yelling felt good. I stomped back to my suite, blood pumping for what felt like the first time in days, with Midge trotting along excitedly behind me.

The next fifteen minutes or so I spent having an imaginary argument with Del in my mind, complete with effusive hand gestures—great fun, I must say. Then, feeling properly prepared for our upcoming verbal sparring, I got bored and messed around with the mirror. Joanna had given me instruction on how to use it yesterday, and after some futzing with the controls I managed to make myself look absolutely demonic: skin pale as paper, pupilless eyes that glowed like blue flame, dark hair that floated about my head in Medusa-like tendrils. The look matched today's outfit well; in keeping with my sour mood, I was looking positively goth in an asymmetrical, gray burn-out tunic (Yohji someone or other) and leather-look leggings (Helmet Wang, I think Joanna had said). I grinned at myself in the mirror and shivered in delight at my teeth, all elongated, pointy, and red.

Maybe there was something to be said for ocular augmentation after all.

Twenty more minutes passed, with neither hide nor hair of Del. "And what is *the master's* ETA?" I asked Joanna at last. I was sitting at the table, struggling through another paragraph of the mystery. I'd deduced whodunnit fifty pages ago.

Her response was a low mumble, her spirals letting off little white sparks of distress.

"What?" I asked.

"Hsntcmng."

"Sorry?"

"H-he's not coming. Perhaps tomorrow?"

I drummed my nails on the table. If I'd been looking in my magic mirror, they would have looked like three-inch long black talons.

So this was to be war, then. And since Joanna's whole reason for existence was to always be there for Del, supporting him, I knew she'd be no ally in this battle.

I heaved a big, dramatic sigh. "I guess that's just how it's going to be between us."

"You'll have to forgive him; he's quite busy."

"Oh, sure, I get it. Big ship like this… I'm sure he has a lot to attend to."

"He *does*," she said, her spirals relaxing a tad. "I know it can be frustrating. Give him some time, and I'm sure you two will be able to get better acquainted."

"Right," I said. "Sure. You know, it's been difficult making the adjustment to living here, so I just got in a bit of a mood there." I shook my head. "Brings me back to when I was younger. I was kind of an angry kid."

"Were you?" she asked, her voice all sympathy. Someone was eager to get off the topic of Del.

"Yeah. Well, my mom died when I was young, and it was pretty tough for a while, getting used to her being gone."

"Aww…" cooed Joanna. "I'm sorry you had to go through that."

I shook my head, looking wistfully away. "Music made it easier. I used to…" I gave a laugh. "I used to listen to the saddest, angriest crap on my boombox. Cranked it up loud, just really wallowed in it, you know? And I think I even knew it was crap, but it still did the trick."

Her usual orange sprouted little green threads: curiosity. "You wouldn't want to listen to some music right now?"

Ding, ding, ding.

"I mean, maybe. Or… you know, could you make me a boombox? And a couple CDs? I know it's just dumb nostalgia, but maybe it would help."

The green threads shifted to an excited purple. I heard noise from the direction of the fabricator; she was already on the case. "Sure. Any album requests?"

I listed off a couple, then had some more fun with the mirror while she worked. A pair of dark, wicked horns added the crowning touch to the whole ensemble. I'd have to find out from Joanna how to save this look for future use.

But first to the task at hand. The fabricator dinged; when it opened, I was met by the smell of warm, newly minted plastic.

What I'd told Joanna hadn't been a total lie. I really had been an angry kid after my mom had died, and I really had tried to drown that anger in music sometimes. In my memories, that whole period of my life was accompanied by a steady stream of angst-ridden albums: Radiohead, My Chemical Romance, Evanescence.

AC/DC hadn't featured in the line-up. But they had featured on a BuzzFeed article I'd read last month about the loudest bands on the planet, and so it was with astounding pleasure that I slotted their album into the boombox, cranked the volume up to full blast, and hit play.

The famous guitar riff roared out from the speakers, shattering the hush of the room. Next came the drums, every beat like a gunshot. Midge rocketed up from the bed, and Joanna went electric white, then a rich, inky blue. Her fractals squirmed like one of those old music visualizers; she was saying something to me, but no way could I hear it—and with the battery-operated boombox, the ruckus was here to stay.

I must have heard my dad play "Highway to Hell" about a million times, but I'd never truly appreciated the defiant, whining scream of the lead singer's vocals. I danced about in the middle of the room, wild as a banshee (which was probably what I looked like, given the current settings of my mirror filters). As the song came to its close, I punched the repeat button, then herded Midge into the bedroom and shut the door to lock her in. It wouldn't be good for her to be present for this next part.

Finally, with a grim little smile to myself, I faced my chair towards the door, sat down primly, and waited. *Bellicose*—that was the word Joanna had used to describe human beings. Such a pretty-sounding word, in contrast to its meaning: an inclination for war.

I'd give them bellicose. I was a person—and not only that, but a red-blooded *American*, God damn it, and I was pretty sure that suffocation by boredom, with only a dog and an AI for company, classified as cruel and unusual punishment. So now that Del had brought me aboard, he was going to have to deal with me: a girl from a line of tough people who lived in a land steeped in God, guns, and rock 'n' roll. (And yes, I knew that AC/DC was an Australian band, but they were serving their purpose well.) Obviously the best result would be an early release for bad behavior, but I'd be happy just to be a thorn in his side—a very loud and annoying thorn.

America, fuck yeah, and all that.

It didn't take long. One second I was mouthing along to the lyrics, and the next Del was looming in the doorway. He looked just as he had when I'd last seen him: dark pants that cut off at the knee, thick, slightly lumpy strap across the chest. His gaze went first to the boombox before darting over to me. Had that been a slight recoil? I wished I could see my demon-self through his eyes.

He shouted something at me, and I waggled my fingers at him in a little wave before pointing to my ear. *Sorry, can't hear you!*

He snarled at me, the muscles in his face tensing, catlike, before he strode over to the boombox. To his credit, he didn't chuck it across the room or attempt to smash it to smithereens.

(That had been my expectation, given his previous behavior toward my dog.) I watched in amusement as he stabbed at the buttons, trying to shut it off; the bass ratcheted way up, then the CD skipped to the next track, then with some final fumbling he found the right button and the song died. Even with the sudden departure of the music, the room seemed to ring with the echo of guitars, like the band had moved on to some other part of the ship, practicing just out of earshot. I wondered if I'd done any permanent damage to my eardrums.

"You look ridiculous," he said, turning to me.

"In my culture," I replied, leaning back in the chair, "it's rude to comment on a woman's appearance. Then again, you wouldn't know anything about that, since you don't give a shit that someone else besides you is living on this ship."

I heard a gasp—Joanna. She was still a deep, appalled blue. "I do apologize for the interruption, master," she said in a quick, tense voice. "I didn't anticipate she—"

"Quiet," he barked, and I stood from the chair in a rush.

"Rude again," I said wonderingly as I walked towards him. I jerked my head towards Joanna. "She's been pretty mum on all things Del, but I gather you're some kind of bigwig." Hopefully whatever magic translation tech he was using to converse in English could handle a word like that. "So it's possible," I continued, stabbing a finger toward his chest, "you're in the habit of bossing people around, ignoring all the little people, but I kind of think you owe me a lot of courtesy, what with, I mean, basically kidnapping me. And I get that this isn't entirely your fault, but then again, you were the one who touched down in our woods. So my *wild* suggestion is that, one, you learn some manners, and two, you drag yourself out of your hidey-hole downstairs every once in a while so we can get to know each other."

I was practically foaming at the mouth by the time I got all the words out. So the speech had sounded cornier spoken aloud than in my head—who cared? At least I'd said my piece.

Del was looking at me with a laser focus, like we were competing in a staring contest. Seconds ticked by. I hadn't seen him since that first day, and his lithe, predatory otherness had dimmed in my memory. Now, gazing up at him, a trickle of fear joined my anger. Was this the part where he decided, *fuck it, best get rid of this one—she's just too annoying?* A creature like Del could snap my spine just like that, I had no doubt.

"Then speak," he growled at last.

"What?"

"You'd like us to come to know each other? Speak. Your kind cannot engage in telepathic communication, so far as I've been told."

It was like someone trying to clear the air after an argument by remarking how quiet everyone else was. I'd always hated those kinds of people.

"How about dinner?" I asked. I'd taken an anthropology class in high school, and I remembered the teacher remarking that a shared meal was a critical component to homo sapiens' bonding rituals. Perhaps that held true with extraterrestrial cultures as well. "I understand you're busy with…" Actually, I had no idea with what. "You're busy. But I'm sure you eat some-times, so let's have a meal together." I'd been about to tack *each day* at the end of that sentence, but decided at the last second that I'd better see how the first meal went before roping myself into a nightly dinner with the king of surly.

He looked so astounded that you might have thought I'd said, *let's go cliff diving, then gallivant in the nude under the gib-bous moon*. "A meal?"

"Yes." I restrained myself from sinking into my talking-with-a-difficult-customer register. We were already on rocky footing. "We could make it a traditional meal, if you'd like. I'm curious to try that. Say, in an hour?"

Another astonished moment passed before he dipped his head in apparent assent. "That would be acceptable."

I'd take acceptable. "All right, then!" I said brightly. "I suggest we eat upstairs, on the top deck. It has such a lovely view."

"Fine," he said with a brusque nod, before turning on his heel and stalking from the room. I breathed a little sigh, resigning myself to what seemed likely to be a very one-sided conversation.

"You tricked me," said Joanna when he was gone. She sounded wounded, and her colors had dimmed.

"Desperate times. I'm sorry." Not altogether true—ends justify the means, et cetera, et cetera—but I'd been raised to be polite.

I went to let Midge out of the bathroom. I didn't trust her to behave around Del, and who could blame her? When she'd bitten him, she'd just thought she was protecting me. It was a side of my sweet dog wholly foreign to me, and I knew I'd have to get to mending the broken fences between them. If Del and I were going to be spending any sort of time together, it wouldn't do for her to want to rip his throat out.

As she sniffed around the room for public enemy number one, I turned to Joanna and clapped my hands together. "Now I don't want this to be a complete disaster. Could you fill me in on the dining customs of Del's people?" More flashbacks to anthropology class: did they use utensils? Did they only eat with one hand? I got the feeling that all the food Joanna had been serving me these past few days had been made with some consideration to my earthly sensibilities, like Americanized Chinese food.

Joanna sank into encyclopedia mode as I walked back to the mirror and swiped away the glamour. The demonic guise had been fun, but I thought it would set a better foundation for cross-cultural understanding to show up to dinner as myself, fresh-faced. My outfit seemed too serious for the occasion; I swapped the dark monotone of the shirt and leggings for a dusky pink wrap dress I'd worn a couple days ago. I paired the dress with some gold flats, then took off the morganite neck-lace. It was simply too pretty. This was a dinner for the purpose of preserving my sanity, not a date.

I still had time to spare, so I brought Midge over to the hot-house for a walk, as Joanna continued the crash course on alien dining. Utensils: yes. Importance of the table's seating arrange-ment: very. Adding condiments or spices to taste: gauche. Fam-ily-style dishes: yes, with a complicated hierarchical system of who could eat what first. After Joanna had explained the rules to me three times, I told her I got it (I didn't), and that we'd best move on.

For a formal meal, the chef might select an incense to burn in the middle of the table that would complement the flavors, like pairing white wine with fish. Psychoactive beverages—the most popular was a cider-like substance called *maht*—were saved for after the meal, as the taste of the drink was considered to distract from the flavors of the food. Sometimes live (!) dishes featured on the menu; Joanna extolled the subtle taste of a mouthful of live *klinvar* as I considered whether it was too late to back out of this meal. Unfortunately, she told me, they couldn't currently offer klinvar on the menu, as the fabricators couldn't make living creatures, and the ship's remaining klinvar stock was much depleted and needed time to breed.

"But maybe you can try them in a couple weeks, once we build their numbers back up," she told me.

"That's all right," I said, repressing the urge to gag. "If they're such a delicacy, it'd be better to save them for someone who'll appreciate them."

Then it was back to my room to deposit Midge; her eyes were forlorn as I shooed her through the door and locked her in. This was the first time I would be willingly venturing anywhere on the ship without her.

Tension pricked at my skin like invisible gnats as I turned away from the door. All the dining facts were smushing together in my mind, the same kind of feeling you get cramming for a test. I sank back against the door, feeling like I was at the very edge of a cliff. Wouldn't it be nice to linger here a bit longer, to make sure I was really, properly prepared…

No. I pushed off the door and stomped down the hall toward the elevator before apprehension could root me in place. The status quo equaled slow suffocation of my mind; something had to give, and if my leaving the *Huivnarrut* was not a possibility, then that something was Del's preference for seclusion.

Stockholm syndrome, my subconscious whispered as I touched a finger to the elevator panel. *You're going to hang out with your captor, and that is dumb, dumb, dumb.* The door whisked open, and I got on, willing my subconscious to kick rocks. Tug of war is not such a fun game when your opponent is your own mind.

But I didn't have to play for long. The elevator doors opened, and I stepped out with my head held high, even if my mind was a tangled, confused mess.

Here I was, Corinne Kaminski, resident human and ready for dinner.

Chapter Eleven

HE'D CLEARED THE SCATTERED FURNITURE FROM THE CENTER of the room and set up a table and chairs for just the two of us.

An unexpected smell floated in the air—light notes of musk, something vaguely citrus-like. I spotted a little golden bowl on the table, its contents letting off wisps of smoke. That would be the incense.

Del stood at the far side of the room, gazing out westward toward the mountains. The day was heading towards twilight, and the peaks were a misty purple in the gathering shadows. He turned to look at me, but stayed where he was by the window. He was straight-backed, stiff.

I walked over and joined him there, keeping a healthy distance between us. I still wasn't used to the sight of him. Do you know that off-guard feeling that steals over you when you see an animal do something really human? That was how I felt around Del at all times; he was so utterly *not* of this world, but the way he moved, talked, walked… There was common ground here, and it tempered his alienness.

"What do you think?" I asked, gesturing towards the scenery.

"It's very… white."

I almost laughed—didn't. Of all the things to say! "Is your world very different?" I didn't even know what his world was called. I didn't even know what his *species* was called. This meeting was long overdue.

He shifted on his feet a little. "From here on Earth? Yes and no." For a second I thought he was going to leave it there, but then he waved a hand at the mountains. My eyes caught on his nails, black and pointed. "Everything here is so dazzling. I find it difficult to look at, often."

I frowned. "What do you mean?"

"The color of the foliage, the sky… It's brighter on Earth. Blue sky where I'm from is an atmospheric abnormality. We rarely get such sunny days as you have here."

"What about snow?"

"No, hardly ever. The snow was a complicating factor the day you came. I believe you were told that by Kh—" He paused, eyeing me.

Ah, so he'd heard about that. "Joanna?" I supplied, and he gave me a terse nod. "Yes, she mentioned it. The hothouse plants are all red and purple," I said, not wanting to lose the conversation thread about his planet. "That's typical, where you're from?"

"Correct," he said. "Owing to a peculiarity with our planet's atmosphere millions of years ago. It limited the light spectrum available to plants."

"What's it called?" I asked, drawing away from the window.

His head tilted. "The… atmospheric peculiarity?"

"No," I said with a soft laugh as I walked towards the table. For better or worse, I was getting hungry. "Your planet."

"Ah. In my language, *Tenctah*."

"Tenctah," I repeated. "And what about your people? Your… species?" Was people a human-centric term? English might not possess enough breadth for the needs of first-contact communications.

"Tenctah has multiple nations," he said, sitting down at the table (in the seat facing the elevator that I'd predicted he'd take, thanks to Joanna's teaching). "Mine," he went on, "is called *Ailopt*." He pronounced this *I lopped*, as in, "I lopped off my enemy's arm in battle, then beat him over the head with it." Somehow I had no difficulty picturing Del doing that very thing.

"And my species is called the *rumae*," he continued. (*ROO-may* was how he said it.)

I repeated that word as well, and something in his face changed. Surprise? Could it be that this experience was just as strange for him as it was for me?

I took my own seat at the table. "Joanna told me about the incense," I said, waving a hand over the bowl to waft some of the smoke in my direction. "It smells quite good."

"Because it is the finest quality Ailoptian money can buy," he said, with palpable pride. Then he threw back his head and roared.

It wasn't exactly a big cat kind of roar, but there was something of that nature mixed in. Evan had shown me a video one time of a bunch of New Zealand rugby players performing a Maori ceremonial battle dance called the haka. The purpose of the haka, Evan explained to me, was to let the enemy know exactly how fucked they were, and I could well imagine Del's roar fitting in well with the routine.

"The server's going deaf," Del said by way of explanation when he lowered his head and saw my stunned expression. A second or two later, I heard an oncoming whirring sound and turned around in my seat to see a squat little robot, looks-wise a close cousin to the cleaner bots, rolling out of the elevator, its arm attachment bearing a tray laden with food. The smell of everything in combination was… bizarre. Not repellent, thanks in part to the incense, but it still didn't smell like anything I had ever put in my mouth. Strange spices warred with unknown sauces clashed with mystery meats. My instincts had been right; Joanna had been dumbing down the food.

Del and I waited as the robot lovingly laid the dishes on the table; when it was done, it gave a satisfied little beep and whirled back to the elevator. Then we watched each other, like two gunslingers about to have a classic Western showdown, hands at our pistols/cutlery. Who was going to draw first? I was furiously trying to wrangle all the hierarchical rules in my mind. What took ultimate precedence? Del was not only my host, but also a host of some significant, undisclosed social ranking. Yet at the same time, I was not only his guest, but also his sole guest, which should secure me a couple points, too—right? Joanna had told me that being female normally placed you up a rung in the dining order, though my pleb status counted against me here. Plus I was an alien species—did that have to be taken into consideration? I had just about worked out an answer when Del let out a low, exasperated noise.

"Eat," he said, waving a hand at the food.

"But I thought—"

"Eat," he urged me again. "In our culture, it would be custom that you would be the one to eat first, of the meat dish most appealing to you."

Damn, I'd done the social math wrong. As he watched on, I surveyed the dishes, looking for a meat dish that called to me.

It was a tough decision, for all the wrong reasons. There was a bowl of what looked like rukla slathered with an oily, vibrant green sauce. There was a large plate of raw-looking bits and bobs—hearts, maybe, or kidneys?—laid out like charcuterie. There was a smaller plate of a pale grilled meat in cubed chunks, half of it glistening, translucent fat.

Seeing me hesitate, Del motioned toward the last dish. "That would be my choice."

Well, okay, I guess it would be my choice, too. "Sure," I said, then found the "fork" (just two tines) and speared one of the chunks.

It was all right. The meat had a sweet smokiness to it that put me in mind of bacon, the fatty portion melt-in-your-mouth, though the idea of eating that much fat in one go held a certain gross-out factor.

"It's good," I said with a nod, like someone might sample a wine and motion for the sommelier to pour the rest of the glass. Per Joanna this was the next bit of the dinner ritual; approval by the first taster allowed everyone else to chow down.

"Lying to me is illegal, you know," he said.

I couldn't help raising an eyebrow. "Is it now?"

"Under Ailoptian law, prevarication in my presence is a criminal offense." He was looking at me with attention, waiting to see how I'd take that bit of information.

I reached forward very deliberately for another piece of whatever it was and gave him a close-lipped smile. "Then it's a good thing I'm American, not Ailoptian. Just in case I ever feel like prevaricating. But I wasn't kidding; the food's not awful. Give me a bit of startup cash and I'll open up Montana's very first Ailoptian-fusion restaurant. We'll do takeout. I'm sure it will be a hit."

He took a heaping spoonful of a stark white, grainy substance—a rice equivalent, if I had to guess—then ladled the green-sauced rukla on top. "I have no idea what you're talking about."

"Don't worry about it. Anyway," I said, following his lead with the grain and rukla combo, "I can't imagine that law stops people lying to you."

He drew back a little. "What makes you say that?"

"You're clearly someone important. I don't know what you're doing here on Earth all alone, but I bet when you're with people they're lying to you left, right, and center. That's what people do with the rich and famous. What is it that you do? Are you a celebrity? Or some sort of entrepreneur?" Maybe he'd invented these robots. Maybe he was the alien equivalent of Elon Musk.

A second ticked by before he opened his mouth. Then he said, a bit stiffly, "I'm the heir apparent."

My hand paused mid-reach for a plate of crimson carrot look-alikes. "What?"

"The heir apparent. To the Ailoptian throne."

For once I had no quippy response. "You're… royal?"

"That's correct."

I eyed him over the table. "So eventually you'll be… King Del?"

"Something like that." He paused. "We use the word *khinahar*, instead of…"

"King."

"Yes."

"Khinahar," I repeated. "Hm."

"The original root of the word means something like…" His eyes unfocused a little as he hunted for the right word. "Exalted."

Jesus Christ. No wonder he strutted around so high and mighty. "So Khinahar Del? Do you have a longer name than that?"

As soon as he drew a breath I knew it was going to be a long one. "Vra-khinahar Zevrae Inu'unt Tox Sharbrit Delklor."

"Whew," I said, exhausted just listening to that never-ending string of syllables, then asked him to say it again, which he did. I gave it a try and got lost halfway through the second name. He took me through it once more, and this time I stumbled to the finish line. It might have been the darkening room fooling me, but I could have sworn his eyes crinkled slightly at the corners.

"Your pronunciation," he said, "is, as you say, not awful."

I waggled my fork at him. "Now don't go prevaricating with me."

He dipped his head toward me and gave me a ghost of a smile. "I would not dare."

We ate in silence for a minute. I was surprisingly digging the red almost-carrots, which had a pickled taste; at last I'd discovered a food here I could honestly say I enjoyed.

"So you're the khinahar—"

"*Vra*-khinahar," he corrected. "As I am still only the heir apparent."

"Okay. Vra-khinahar. But once you become the khinahar, is that mostly a position where you, er, rule? Or is it just a… a ceremonial thing?" Like the Queen of England, whose main role, as far as I could tell, was to show off her plentiful collection of showy, monochromatic hats.

He let out a slight guttural noise that almost—almost!—sounded like a laugh. "It's a position of the highest power. In addition to the khinahar, Ailopt does have a ruling body of officials, but they ultimately submit to the khinahar's authority." His mouth tightened. Whatever amusement he'd shown a moment ago seeped away. "I will rule."

"Then excuse my curiosity, but what the hell are you doing in Wakpa, Montana? Shouldn't you be back on Tenctah, doing… vra-khinahar stuff?"

His gaze flicked over to the window; the sun had gone down while we'd been eating, and the sky was a deepening blue. The glass of the ceiling overhead, completely transparent in the daytime, was now lit up with delicate lights that twinkled like the pinprick of distant stars. They illuminated the room with a ghostly silver glow.

"A fair question," he said. "Of course, much of my work can be handled while I'm off-planet."

"Er—sure. But why—?"

He was back to looking out the window, and now he stood up swiftly. "Thank you for the pleasant conversation."

"Aren't you hungry? You've hardly eaten anything." I hadn't even seized my chance yet to put food on his plate—something Joanna had told me was a critical part of any traditional meal, meant to demonstrate respect between the diners.

"The time grows late," he said. "I have duties that lie elsewhere this evening." Then he inclined his head toward me sharply and left me sitting there at the table without a word of goodbye. Behind me, the elevator door swooshed open, then closed. Joanna must be here with me—I was sure she'd heard the whole conversation—but she was keeping quiet.

I finished eating in silence, as Del's half-full plate went untouched. I was a bit baffled. Surely I'd committed some gaffe to cause him to leave like that, but even after going over all the dining rules in my head again, I couldn't pinpoint my offense.

Or maybe he was just sensitive, though I couldn't imagine about what. And if not sensitive, then certainly secretive. What *was* he doing hovering above Wakpa? Alien invasion was the obvious, disturbing thought, but would the aliens really commence their assault in Montana? I shook my head at the spread of food before me, now growing cold.

Me, though… I'd been dragging through these few days on the ship in a state of numb torpor. Now, despite Del's strange exit, I felt the slightest touch warmer than I had the entire time I'd been on board, like something frozen inside me had lost its outermost shell of ice. Funny how the mere act of talking could do that—even talk with an extraterrestrial.

"I hope you're happy with yourself," Joanna said in a miffed tone as I came back into the room. Midge was at my side in a flash, ecstatic.

"I am," I said, bending to give Midge a hug.

"Was it a pleasant evening?"

"Very pleasant," I answered, somewhat truthfully. "I *am* sorry for deceiving you."

"But you're still going to do it again, though, aren't you? With the boombox?"

"Oh yes." I had a nice selection of CDs, courtesy of Joanna, and since the boombox was still in working order I was definitely going to make use of them. "I know you don't approve, and I'm sorry for using you, but it's my one tool for getting out of solitary."

She didn't reply, just pulsed gently at me with a mix of amber and turquoise. "All right," she said eventually. "I understand."

Not that she approved—but at least that she understood. I'd take that. "Thank you. Now how about some bedtime reading?"

"Sure," she said, her tone a touch less frosty. Since we both enjoyed Jane Austen, she'd been reading *Emma* aloud to me. Myself, I wasn't as big on *Emma* as *Pride and Prejudice*, but I still liked listening to Joanna read; with her beautiful English accent, she had a great voice for audiobook narration.

"Where were we again?" I asked her.

"Chapter Seven. Remember how Frank Churchill hared off to London for a mere haircut?"

"Right, I remember now." *A sudden freak*, as Austen put it, *seemed to have seized him at breakfast.*

A sudden freak… I thought back to Del standing suddenly from the table. I now knew worlds more about him and his planet, Tenctah. But as for why he had navigated the *Huivnar-rut* from Ailopt—however far away that was—to set up camp just outside the confines of my backyard, that answer remained hidden. Del had a secret, he was sensitive about it, and I wanted to know it.

Chapter Twelve

When I checked my garden the next morning I knew there was a problem. There were all sorts of reasons I'd anticipated my little plot of vegetables not going to plan: foreign microbes, the wrong soil pH, an overly moist environment, the twilit conditions. But my plants were fine—*more* than fine. The onions were already three inches tall, their shoots oddly thick and beefy. The jalapenos measured in at a whopping five inches—*five inches* after being in the ground just a few days— and the tomatoes weren't far behind. I could smell the spice of their leaves from two feet away.

Plant steroids, I thought, eyeing the dark soil nervously. *I'm growing Plant Godzilla.* Then I cast an even more nervous gaze around me, searching for any glimpse of the wall. If I could see the wall, Joanna could see me, and maybe the plants, too. Their green shone bright as a beacon against the backdrop of reds and purples.

It was hard to make out anything clearly in this dim lighting, so I'd just have to trust that the spot I'd picked really was shrouded from view. Of course, I could just pull them all up and put my worries to rest, but that ran counter to all my plant-loving instincts.

"How's the garden?" Joanna asked when I rejoined her a few minutes later.

"Nada," I said, shaking my head. "But it's early days."

"It normally takes at least a week for onions to sprout," she said, deepening to warm amber: Joanna the know-it-all. "Tomatoes, too. Just give it a bit, I'd say."

My skin itched. This was a dangerous game I was playing, my opponent a supercomputer. "Yeah, I'll give it a bit," I echoed as I exited the hothouse. "Probably they won't even sprout at all, but you never know."

Back in my room, I selected "It's Oh So Quiet" as this morning's summoning bell. I could have waited for dinnertime, but the ship had a hush about it that morning that begged to be broken, and besides, I felt like a good scream.

Del burst through the door on my third repeat of the song. "Why," he shouted over the tranquil, lullaby-like midsection, "are you *shrieking?*"

"Not me," I said, flashing him a great big grin as I went to lower the volume before the big band could get going again. "Björk. She's always struck me as a bit alienish herself, so I thought you might enjoy—"

"It's terrible," he said, shaking his head at me in dismay. "It's *uncivilized.* Do humans really listen to such music for pleasure?"

Oh, zing boom. That was rich, coming from the guy who had chucked my poor dog around and liked to roar at robots.

"I'll get you hooked on Earth music," I said. "Just give me a week or two. Now, are you hungry? I thought we could enjoy breakfast together on the top deck."

"I—"

"Because I'm pretty hungry myself, and I'd love to see what an Ailoptian breakfast spread is like. If you do eat breakfast, that is."

He regarded me silently, perhaps wondering how he'd wound up saddled with this particular human, out of all seven billion plus of us.

"Please," I said. "Then you can go back to whatever." That last bit was a fib, but no need to worry about it just this second. I'd get some food in the both of us first before revealing my other plans for the day.

I could see the moment when he caved: a softening around the eyes, a relaxing around his mouth. Soon I'd be able to read him just as well as any other human.

"Fine," he barked. "Breakfast." He relayed a message in his language to Joanna, who had been observing all this with wriggling blue tendrils of worry. Then to me: "Ten minutes. Top deck." I was sorely tempted to salute with an "Aye aye, captain," but managed to contain myself. After yesterday's excitement and now this, I might be pushing the limits of my Ailoptian host's patience.

He left the room in his usual stiff-backed way. Was this a rumae mannerism? Or something to be chalked up to heir-apparent behavior? Maybe tonight I'd ask Joanna to give me a lesson in rumae etiquette—or, better yet, I'd figure out a time to give Del a lesson in human etiquette. Not today, because I had a different scheme in mind, but soon.

I took a minute to spruce up in my magic mirror, then dragged Midge to the hothouse for a quick walk before heading upstairs. Today Joanna had made me a pair of floral silk palazzo pants and an off-shoulder, cherry-blossom pink bodysuit, both straight from Oscar de la Renta's upcoming spring collection. My hair was still drying from my morning bath, and I quickly roped it into a side braid to give the length nice waves later, then slid in a small diamond clip at the top for some sparkle. I finished off the outfit with a pair of cream kidskin pumps (Jimmy Choo) with a heel I could just barely manage.

I was feeling, in a word, fine.

The room upstairs was awash with sunlight. It was one of those rare, blue-sky winter days, and I could see for miles in any direction. Snow dusted the trees and mountain tops like powdered sugar. I didn't let my gaze drift homeward.

Del was already waiting for me by the table, and he took a seat as I drew nearer. The table was laid with food; the server bot had already been and gone. No incense today. I inspected the foods: a few meat dishes, a bowl of small, gray speckled eggs, a platter of green and yellow fruit slices dotted with little black seeds.

"Do rumae not bake?" I blurted, with the sudden realization that I had yet to see a single dough-based foodstuff.

"Bake?" His brow creased.

"You know—cookies? Cakes? *Bread?*" He just looked even more confused. "Oh no," I said, shaking my head. "You poor,

poor…" *Man?* Again, my English vocabulary was a bit lacking for this scenario. "…rumae," I finished.

"Those are foods?" His translation abilities must be struggling.

I nodded as I filled my plate. "That's right. Not the healthiest thing to eat, but they're delicious."

He huffed a sort of scoffing noise. "I'm told that humans don't seem to mind a bit of destruction for fleeting happiness."

Oh, was that the way it was? "Did you read that in some sort of field guide? I'm sure rumae are just the same."

"Perhaps."

"Definitely. You're just not seeing the forest for the trees."

"The forest?" He looked to the window questioningly.

"Never mind," I said, flapping my hand. Then I took a bite of a cold sausage that tasted strangely of black olives, arranged my mouth into a winning smile—I hate olives—and motioned for him to dig in.

"Tell me of yourself," he said as he began to load his plate, catching me off guard. "Your life. What you enjoy doing."

I won't pretend I wasn't completely shocked. This most solitary of aliens, inquiring about little old me? Probably he wanted to avoid more of my prying.

Where to start? "Well," I said, straightening up, "I'm pretty ordinary. My full name is Corinne Eleanor Kaminski—Eleanor for my grandaunt, my father's grandmother's sister. I've lived here in Wakpa all my life." And my favorite color is pink and my favorite ice-cream flavor is candy cane. No, he surely didn't care about those standard icebreaker tidbits.

"My family are very regular people," I said, wondering if that counted for anything with an alien prince. "Er, commoners, I guess. Except for you, I've never met anyone who's royal. I mean, it makes sense that I haven't met anyone royal because I live in the United States. Don't be offended, but we Americans historically aren't big on royalty. We're a federal republic." God, I had fully boarded the babble train now, but Del still seemed to be giving me his full attention. Or maybe he had just perfected his "look interested" expression and was actually zoning out, thinking about his more pressing heir-apparent duties. That was the sort of thing I assumed a vra-khinahar had to get good at.

"And what do you do?" he prompted me. "Do you have a job? A spouse? Children?"

"N-no children," I said, flushing. "And no husband. I work in a kayak-and-ski shop. It's not a glamorous job, but I enjoy it."

"Kayak and ski…"

"You don't know what those are?"

"Kayaking is…" He eyes drifted away and his nose wrinkled. "…something to do with a small boat?"

"That's right. And skiing is where you use, um, skis—these long flat things—to move over snow. People think it's fun. It's also a great way to break a leg, which was how I broke my leg when I was twelve. I like kayaking a lot more. Behind the shop where I work there's a river called the Big D—er, the Big Deer River, so when the weather's good I kayak down it a lot."

"You enjoy outdoor recreational activities," he said slowly, not like he was asking a question but more like he was taking notes on some complex topic.

"Yes," I said, waving a hand toward the windows. "I live in a beautiful place. It would be a crime not to."

"And you own a… kayak-and-ski shop."

"Well, no. I don't own it. I just work there for the owner, Ray. But I do have more responsibilities than most of the other employees. Ray counts on me for a lot of things."

He gave a short nod. Responsibilities and duties—this seemed to be an easy concept. "What will this Ray do now that you won't be working for him any longer?"

I looked down at my plate. I'd hardly gotten in a bite to eat so far, since I'd been doing all the talking. "It's not like my role is that difficult. I-I'm expendable. He'll promote someone else, and life will continue."

"But you enjoy this career as a shopgirl."

More heat rose in my cheeks. "Yes. I do."

Thankfully he moved on to other topics. "And what else of the rest of your life? Are you schooled?" His intonation was much the same way you'd ask someone if their dog was house-trained.

"Yes, I am," I said, setting my fork down. I wasn't going to be getting much eating done, clearly. "I graduated from high school with honors. And I've taken some college classes, but I haven't finished up." Wasn't even close, as a matter of fact, but "haven't finished up" was how I usually phrased it, for my ego's sake. I hadn't even registered for the coming semester.

"College," he said, and I could see him parsing the word.

"It's a… place of higher learning. Students delve into topics in depth, most frequently in group classes."

"Thanks for clarifying that for the both of us. Ailoptians don't go to college or university?"

His head flicked a bit to the side, like a bee had just flown by his ear. Yet more body language for me to learn. "No, we do…" He searched for the proper English word. "…apprenticeships. Something similar to that. What did you study?" he asked, barreling on before I could press him further.

"Biology, with a botany focus." The words stung my mouth. "I mean, that was the plan. I didn't get very far."

"And you've no other family, besides your father? No romantic prospects?"

Essentially, *what kind of a loser are you?* Or maybe that was just me projecting. He was looking at me like a thing to be studied and analyzed from every angle, his gaze steady and… nonjudgmental? I had a right to be irritated at this point, but it just wasn't coming to me.

"Not currently," I said in answer to his question. "Romantic prospects, I mean. And my family's pretty small, and we don't get together all that often, since we're spread out across the country. I'm an only child, and my mom died when I was young, so it's really just my dad and me."

His head jerked back a little. Joanna hadn't told him, though she could have. "How did she die?"

"A car accident," I said in a softer voice. "It was a sudden thing. She didn't suffer." I had suffered—for a long, long time I had suffered—but at least she had not.

"On Tenctah," said Del, "personal and commercial vehicles maneuver automatically. Only some emergency vehicles and those for sport are driven manually. Collisions are quite rare."

Well, whoopty-do and good for Tenctah. I could feel that missing spark of irritation coming on now, *real* strong.

"But," he continued, "I read once about the fatalities from the era of manually operated vehicles. The details were terrible. Shocking. I am sorry for your loss."

I gave him the barest nod, then we took a few minutes in silence to eat. The fruit slices were delicious, a bit like a sugar-sweet strawberry, and the little eggs were exactly as they looked, cooked to a soft-boiled consistency (the yolks a ruby red, though). Maybe I could get ahold of them in raw form so I could make an omelet.

Del sat back in his seat as I finished off the last bit of fruit. "Your thoughts?" he asked, with a glance down at my plate.

"Tasty," I said, then blinked as I remembered something. "Oh, I'm supposed to… I forgot…" I reached for a slice of the olive-flavored sausage with my fork and, with some hesitation, brought it towards his plate. Nerves made my hand jerk, causing the sausage slice to leap from the fork and land in a tumble on his plate, right in the middle of a little puddle of fruit juice. I gave him a weak smile; he was looking at me with what seemed to be shock.

"Joanna told me— She said it was a sign of respect…"

He roared, not for the robot this time, but with a resounding bark of laughter that bounced all around the room.

I frowned. "I only thought I would—"

"No!" he said, chuckling. It wasn't an entirely human sort of chuckle—a bit rougher, more in the chest than the throat—but still a chuckle all the same. And his lips had curved upward and broken apart in an alarming manner. Very toothy. "Just the way that—in terms of execution, it was not the best. But thank you."

"In English, we have a saying 'it's the thought that counts,'" I said with a sniff, skewering a piece of fruit.

He mulled that over. "An odd saying. Wouldn't that equate failure with success? Which would encourage mediocrity."

"I suppose?"

"A culture could wither and die by that philosophy."

I'd never thought of it that way before. I guess that was the sort of thing an heir apparent had to keep an eye out for, given that he'd one day head a country. Kingdom? Khinaharship? "Anyway," I said, "if I was so terrible, maybe you could show me how it's really done." I gestured from him to my own plate, then sat back to watch the show.

How it was really done, it turned out, was worlds apart from my sloppy job. He regarded the sausage slices for a moment, before selecting the choicest morsel and scooting it carefully onto the tines of his fork. Then he gently brought it over to my side of the table (*Open up and say ah!*) and laid it on my plate with something akin to reverence. It was a wonder he could hold the fork at all with those long, dark nails, let alone maneuver it so delicately.

"All right," I said, looking from the sausage back up to him. "You win." And now I had to eat the damn thing. Yum, olives.

"You don't like it," he said as I wavered, his eyes squinting—laughing!—at me.

"No, not really," I admitted. "Though I'll pretend I do, for the sake of America and Ailopt's budding intergalactic relations."

He nodded. "Diplomatic of you. In truth, that dish is fabricated, though the fruit and eggs are not. Our ship's fabricators do a decent impression of the real thing, but an impression only."

"Or," I said, my voice dropping to a conspiratorial whisper, "there might be a different culprit."

"Hm?"

"Is she listening?"

He looked flummoxed. "Who?"

"Joanna."

"She is always listening, by default—oh. You mean…?"

"What I mean," I said, "is that perhaps—just perhaps!—Joanna's culinary skills are a bit lacking."

He blinked at me. Then there was a little, strangled noise from the back of his throat. His shoulders shook, followed by a burble of laughter. "It's possible," he agreed after a moment, lips still twitching. "You are really a singular being."

"I'll take that as a compliment. I mean, she tried to make lasagna and apple pie on the first night here." His head did that bee-by-your-ear flick again. "Both of those are pretty normal dishes. And they were slop—probably worse than slop. And that was her very first attempt at human food, I get it, but… all I'm saying is that maybe Joanna has a weakness, and maybe that weakness is food. So no, I don't particularly like… this," I said, with a gesture toward the sausage growing ever more cold on my plate. "But I'd be happy to try the real deal. Provided I get that chance someday. Because I've been worried, you know, that sometime soon we're going to depart from Earth for Ailopt and you'll stick me in a royal menagerie of alien beings. And then I'll only get to eat kibble formulated for human consumption till the end of my days. That isn't what's going to happen to me, is it?"

"No," he said, serious again. "That won't be what happens to you. As a member of an intelligent species, you are afforded your due rights as per our laws. Life will continue for you much as it has on the ship."

"But we will be leaving for Ailopt sometime," I said. "Right?"

His expression grew yet somber. "Yes, that is correct."

I had the sudden sense that we were heading into the same murky territory from last night, so I corrected course. "Well, I'm glad to know I'm not destined for a zoo. That's heartening." I pushed my plate away. "Now how about getting to know my dog?"

Chapter Thirteen

It took some convincing, but I got him in the end. I mean, it had to be done; with just us three corporeal beings on board, it made no sense for two of the three to have a brawl-on-sight relationship.

So after I overruled all Del's protestations (no time, no need, no inclination), I ventured with him back down the elevator to my room, carrying the leftover olive-flavored sausage on a plate. Along the way I gave him a basic breakdown. He was not to approach Midge or move quickly around her. He was to let her sniff him as she liked.

"And I don't think she'll do this, but let her lick you if she wants to."

"*Lick?*"

"Yes. Licking equals dog kisses."

"In Ailopt, our pets—"

"—are far superior, I'm sure. Minimal licking, no hairballs or rummage sessions through the garbage—you can tell me all about it later. Anyway, I doubt Midge will be feeling lovey-dovey." I drew up short before my door. "And like I told you before, the most important thing is the sausage. Food is top of the pyramid for dogs—they really like it, I mean. So we are going to ply her with food, until this whole plate is bare." There was still quite a lot of sausage left on the plate; it seemed neither Del nor I were huge fans of whatever-it-was. Hopefully Midge would have a different opinion.

"All right," I said, touching my finger to the button. "You stay here and—"

But I realized as soon as the door swished open that on my way to breakfast I had neglected to lock Midge in the bathroom. I felt more than saw her rocket past me towards Del with a whoosh of air, and I launched myself toward her like a soccer goalie diving for a ball. What I didn't take into consideration with this maneuver were the Jimmy Choos; the right stiletto heel betrayed me and turned inward, sending me staggering, and I lost hold of the plate. Sausage flew through the air like confetti, landing with little plops on the ground. I could hear much snarling from behind me, my sweet, darling Midge sounding for all the world like a slavering wolf.

"Midge!" I shrieked (along with a few other things) as I worked on righting myself. The heel of my right shoe had broken, leaving me lopsided; I kicked both of the dratted things off, then wrenched around to face the chaos.

Del held my dog aloft at arm's length as she glared and snapped at him. "Give her to me," I shouted, hurrying over and bringing all forty pounds of her squirming muscle into my chest. She didn't look injured and neither did he, thank goodness.

In a way, it was flattering that Midge was so protective of me, but the last thing I wanted was her making a habit of biting people.

"Okay," I said as she struggled against me, every ounce of her being focused on Del. "I'm heading in, and you pick up all of that." I bobbed my head downward toward the sausage. "Then knock when you're ready to come in so I know to hold her real tight."

"I don't think there's any chance—"

"Just knock when you're ready." I, too, had growing doubts that there was any hope of easing this relationship, but we had to try.

Inside the room I sat on the bed, still holding Midge in my arms, and stroked her face soothingly. I could feel her heart pounding pitter-patter through her chest. She let out a high whine, craning her neck towards the door, then huffed a breath of frustration and relaxed into me.

"I know," I murmured in her ear. "But he's really all right— you'll see. Sort of high and mighty, a bit… well, *princely*, but generally okay, I think. Now in a second he's probably going to come in, so you need to be good, Midge." Her eyes rolled in my direction at the sound of her name, still keeping her ears crooked towards the door. The quick beat of her heart had slowed some. "Good girl. So just stay calm and—okay, here we go."

The door opened a second after Del's knock, and Midge's every muscle tensed as she tried to escape my hold. "No sudden movements," I called to him. "Right there's fine." He'd paused just past the threshold of the door; the next step of the plan was for me to come closer. Clutching Midge tight, I approached the enemy. Midge fought me the whole way, squirming like an unruly, furry toddler.

And then I reached him. After some final, desperate thrashing, accompanied by many fearsome noises, Midge sagged and went deadweight, accepting the jail of my arms as her new normal. Her nose, though, was going a mile a minute. It's a wonder that dogs aren't passing out all the time from hyperventilation.

"That's a good girl," I said to her, scooting an inch closer to Del. She loosed another unhappy growl, and with a burst of inspiration I shifted my gaze towards Del. "I'm going to touch you," I said, keeping my voice all calm and cooey for Midge.

"What?"

"Just to let her see you're not going to gobble me up, okay?" And before he had a chance to respond, I adjusted my hold on her so that I had a free hand and reached out for his arm.

My first thought was, *oh, soft*. Of course I'd touched Del previously, that first day when I'd slapped him, and then later that same day when he'd carried me to my room. Yet both of those times I'd been out of my mind from either anger or fear, and now—I don't want to say I had time to *enjoy*, exactly, but at least time to observe. The short, reddish fur covering his skin was sleek, and he felt warmer than a human by a couple degrees. I felt his muscles stiffen. What must I look like to him, all pale and relatively hairless? As alien as a naked mole-rat, probably.

What a lovely, self-affirming thought. I refocused on the task at hand.

"See, Midge?" I gave his arm another little pat. "Nothing to worry about." Then to him: "Okay, give her a piece."

Carefully, carefully he held out a morsel of sausage to her in his palm. Her sniffing revved up, and in a moment of magic, with her eyes fixed on his, she extended her neck. The power food holds over a dog—it's an astonishing thing to behold.

She tentatively took the sausage from him, gumming it as if considering whether to spit it out. Oh God, what if she hated the olive sausage, too? But thankfully she swallowed it down after a moment, then looked to me with bright eyes. Pride surged through me. "Good girl! All right, try another piece."

Over the next few minutes we proceeded to feed her the whole plateful. Maybe the rumae were onto something with this food-sharing thing, since it was charming the she-wolf right out of my dog, hopefully never to be seen again. Somewhere along the way I felt her tail come to life, and I deemed it safe to let her down to the ground. That commenced another sniffing session—his legs, his feet. And his—oh gosh, if there's one thing dogs lack it's a sense of shame. "You can push her away," I said, laughing as he took a startled step backward.

Then he, too, rumbled a laugh and relaxed. "I read about dogs and their sense of smell. But I didn't expect…"

I nodded. "You should see the standard dog greeting sometime. Here, try throwing this for her." I grabbed her tennis ball and tossed it to him; he caught it easily, but his expression was uncertain.

"Just—anywhere?" Midge's eyes were darting back and forth between us, her haunches aquiver for a game of monkey in the middle.

"Anywhere."

He tossed it in the direction of the bathroom, and she bounded after it, returning a few seconds later to drop it at his feet.

"See?" I said. "Now do that eight hundred more times."

He bent to pick up the ball and threw it faster this time, Midge a streak of dark fur in pursuit. "And this is what you do with her, every day?"

"Oh, yeah," I said. "Up and down the hallways. Or sometimes we go up to the top deck, so she really has the space to run."

He was silent for a moment, then grabbed the ball from Midge again. "And what fills the rest of your day?"

I looked away from him. "I take her for walks in the hothouse. I garden. I read or watch TV. I talk with Joanna. And…" Surely there had to be something else? But there wasn't; I was a bird in a gilded cage. "That's pretty much it. Oh, I summon you to eat with annoying music."

"Which you will do tomorrow." His tone was strange, not quite a question. Something lurked there behind the words.

I squinted at him. "Do you… want me to?"

His red eyes glimmered, his lips forming the smallest trace of a smile. "I doubt my wants much factor into your decision. You are a—" His head tilted. "Is that truly the right word? A… steamroller? A type of construction machinery used to flatten surfaces?"

I barked a laugh. "Someday you *have* to tell me how your translation works."

"I could not tell you if I tried."

"All this technology is like magic," I said, tossing the ball for Midge again.

Del nodded solemnly. "Most times it functions flawlessly.

Then there are those times when it makes a mess of my mind." He shuddered. "Idioms and slang have the potential to be dizzying."

I nearly laughed again before I saw his expression. "You're really serious. You mean if I were to say—no, never mind." I wasn't a sadist, after all. "And all this is done with an implanted chip in your brain?"

"Something like that. A concentrated collection of nanobots. It's a routine surgery, performed when most of us are children."

I might be chipless, but this conversation was also making me dizzy. "What's it like talking? That must be strange."

He stroked his throat, grimacing. "The feeling is… mildly alarming. A sudden disconnection from your jaw, lips, and tongue."

"Sounds awful," I said, wrinkling my nose.

"One grows used to it. Mostly."

"Could you say something to me in your language? What's your language even called?"

He said a big mix of syllables.

"Say it again?"

"*Ziryahshun,*" he said, slowing his speech.

"Ziryahshun," I repeated back. "Say something in Ziryahshun. Like, *hello, how are you?*" I hadn't been one for languages in school, but a good part of that was down to my mother's passing. She'd died the year I'd started Spanish class, and the shock and the grief had made it so grades were the last thing on my mind. When the class moved past *hola* and *cómo estás,* I was left fumbling.

"You would say—" And again here he spoke a long string of syllables that I lost halfway through.

Still, I gave it my best. "*Garayoop dee murvit?* No, stop laughing! Say it again!"

We went back and forth a few more times before he deemed my pronunciation passable. Something like *Grrup dih, mahrrvipt,* with much emphasis on the *R*s. Ziryahshun was a language of growls.

Del's next words surprised me. "Say the greeting in English."

"You mean hello?"

"Yuh mee-uhn hahloh?"

He'd switched off his translation. I waved my hands in what I hoped was the intergalactic sign for no. "Hello."

"Hehlowuh."

I gestured for him to try again. "Hello, how are you?"

"Hehlowuh, hah ahrrr yuh."

He could almost have passed for a very tipsy North Dakotan. "Hello, how are you?" I repeated in a kindergarten-teacher cadence.

"Hehloh, howuh ahrr yoo." His accent was better, if only marginally. I gave him a thumbs up, then switched that for an encouraging nod when I realized chances were good he had no idea what thumbs had to do with anything.

He tried the phrase once more, and I kept us going this time. "Good, thanks."

"Guhd, teehnks."

"Good, thanks."

"Goo-uhd, tihnks."

I did a swirly hand motion that I hoped he'd understand to mean, *take it from the top.*

"Hehlah, howuh ahrr yuh?"

"Good, thanks!" I replied, beaming. It might be just a few words, but it still felt like the start of something positive.

Del looked at Midge, who had settled down on the bed for a nap during all this language exchange. "I am glad your dog has decided to abide me. And this interlude has been amusing."

Oh, good, because that's why I was here: for amusement's sake. But I couldn't bring myself to be sarcastic with him; Del might talk like a stuck-up prince sometimes, but he *was* a prince, after all, and a prince in translation at that. "I'm guessing you have to get going?"

Whatever relaxed quality he'd had moments ago was disappearing, flattened under the serious expression he wore like a mask. "Yes."

"Will we eat together again tomorrow?"

He dipped his head. "I will await your terrible musical selection."

I'd thought I was an annoyance to him. When I'd used the boombox to goad Del into talking with me yesterday, I'd come into that conversation furious and prepped for war. But now here we were a few meals later, and the animosity had evaporated away, leaving an odd sproutling of a friendship in its place.

That night, rather than diving back into *Emma*, I asked Joanna to give me a lesson in elementary Ziryahshun.

Chapter Fourteen

I WAS OUT OF BED EARLY THE NEXT DAY. MY MIND WAS A JUMBLE of Ziryahshun phrases that had whispered at me all night through a fog of dreams: *hello*, *goodbye*, *what's your name*, et cetera.

"Grrehlm'ahr," I growled at Joanna, hoping I'd picked the right phrase for our social status differences. *Good morning*.

"Grrehlm noh!" she greeted me back, all curving peaches and purples. "I'm impressed! You're a fast learner."

"Isherrh." *Thanks*. "What's it looking like today?"

The neutral tone of the walls faded away to reveal white mountains and gray skies, like my bedroom was floating in midair. It had snowed the previous night; the trees were heavy with it. My spirits grew heavy, too, at the sight.

What was the date today? Christmas must be right around the corner, and this would be the first year I wouldn't be spending the holiday at home.

"How many days till Christmas?" I asked Joanna, my eyes still tracing the peaks and dips of the mountains. It would be a busy day at the shop today, with everyone in a buying mood and fresh snow on the ground.

"Eight," she answered.

And how many days had it been now since I'd smelled fresh air or felt the kiss of snowflakes on my cheeks? How many more would it be? Walking to the mirror, I examined myself head to toe, without a stitch of clothing. I looked gaunt and pale, like some essence within me was leaking away.

"There's no place on board where I can get a breath of fresh air?" I asked her. "No… no air vent or anything?"

"No," Joanna said softly, her colors fading to washed-out pastel. "We're airtight. It's one reason for the hothouse; the oxygen generated by the plants keeps things fresh."

Ah, yes, airtight—because this was a spaceship, after all.

"Viohr." *Okay.* Then my only choice was to burrow in, to find some solace in my cage.

On our morning walk, I decided it was time to kill my plants. In a span of twenty-four hours they'd gone from husky to freakish—the vegetable version of those juiced-up bodybuilders you see on magazine covers with veins popping. The tomatoes had already flowered and were fruiting yellow-orange globes. I glared down at them. One more day at this pace and they'd be fully ripe—and there was nothing I loved more than homegrown tomatoes.

But no, I couldn't risk Joanna spotting the plants' vibrant green. I plucked the two ripest tomatoes, ate one, and offered the other to Midge, who wolfed it down. Mine was sour, of course, but it was better than nothing.

"Taste like home?" I whispered to her, and she wagged her tail at me before going off to patrol her usual spots.

I had to make quick work of pulling everything up, since I didn't want Joanna to get suspicious, but I did my best to do a thorough job. Leave any of the onions in the ground and I was sure to have a whole hothouse of the stuff in a week. When I was satisfied that I'd thoroughly excised the plants, I brought the whole heap to the gazebo and pushed them way under a seat for concealment. Then I used the inside of my shirt to wipe my hands clean of dirt as best I could.

"You look upset," Joanna said when I joined her at the door.

"Just hoping I'll get some sprouts."

"Nothing yet, then?"

"I mean, it could still take some time…"

"But maybe you could try more seeds, to hedge your bets," she said. "Different varieties? Or plant in a different spot? I could make you a planter. You could put it on the top deck, so the sprouts would get real sunlight." Classic Joanna, eager to whisk away my sadness with fabricated goodies.

I hemmed and hawed. "Maybe in a few days. I just don't want to give up on this batch. I'm thinking the nutrients in the soil are off, but God knows what. Magnesium, potassium, nitrogen, calcium… Or it could be the pH…"

She grew little tendrils of interest, green as the plants presently dying under the gazebo seat. "I'll make you a kit to test the soil."

"Really?" I said. "I mean, I'll be honest, the seeds are probably a lost cause. Maybe I should just start over. The top deck's not a bad idea." I aimed for just the right note of pathetic.

She quivered, her green deepening to jade. "No, no, stop that. I'm already making you a kit; it'll be in the room when you get back. What's the harm in testing the soil?"

I put on a quivery little smile. "Yeah, I guess. That's right. What's the harm?"

A few hours later, after I'd frittered away my morning—breakfast, reading—I took a seat on the floor and riffled through my meager CD collection. I wasn't feeling any of the nostalgic emo spread in front of me; I wasn't even feeling loud. Pulling up the plants had put a sour taste in my mouth, like I was still sucking on the tomato. And there was a definite part of me that was freaking out about my deception, and a small ember, too, that might be hopeful.

I was a tangled mess, and none of the CDs before me were going to straighten me out. But what did that matter, when I had a genius AI as my constant companion?

"Can I hum something to you?" I asked Joanna. "I think it's Chopin something or other. And you'll play it if you can figure out what it is? I just don't know the name."

"Of course."

My mom had only been a so-so cook, but she'd nevertheless been a stickler for family dinners (places set, elbows off the table, sometimes even a candle), and part of that time had been used for my musical edification. While she plated the food, my dad would get some music going. My parents could not have had more different tastes in music—rock for my dad, jazz and classical for my mom, with the occasional eighties one-hit wonder thrown in for good measure.

But mostly she'd stuck to her jazz and classical. I wasn't good at identifying this sonata and that composer, but most of your standard repertoire I could recognize no problem. Now I found a song wandering through my head—solo piano, happy and sad at once, with an air of resignation weighing everything down. I envisioned someone sitting on a hill watching on as their house burned to the ground. "But look at that beautiful sunset," they'd say as they laid back on the hill, once there was no doubt that the house was beyond saving. That was the vision the song had always conjured for me, and it was how I was feeling myself, having killed those plants. My one taste of home, gone.

You take a few steps forward, and maybe you take a few steps backward, too. You kill some vegetables, and you get a soil test kit. What you really need to focus on is that home isn't so far away, and it might not take so many steps forward to make it back.

"That's one of Chopin's nocturnes," Joanna said after a few seconds of my tuneless humming. I have a terrible voice. "Opus nine, number two. Here."

And the song in my head became real, the simple beauty of the piece filling the room. I settled back on the carpet, closed my eyes, and readied myself for a cry. When I'm all at odds inside, there's nothing like a good bout of tears to sort me out.

Halfway through, the door to the room hissed open. There

was only one person it could be. I kept my eyes closed. Maybe he'd think I'd fallen asleep on the floor and go away.

"Corinne?" he growled. No, not growled—that was just his voice. God, everything around me was so foreign, and me the one speck of normalcy. Would this state of affairs never stop bowling me over the head?

"I'm sleeping," I said, rolling over and curling around Midge, who was napping next to me on the carpet. At least I'd solved that problem.

"Er," he said. There was a lengthy pause. Had he gone? Then: "I don't think you are. Unless you're talking in your sleep. Which I am told is sometimes possible for your species, but…" Another silence. "The song is pleasant."

"Pleasant," I echoed into the soft fluff of Midge's fur. "Yes, well, it's not as if Chopin is one of humanity's greatest composers of all time or anything. Maybe I'll play you some Mozart tomorrow—he's *pleasant*. Or Beethoven—that Moonlight Sonata's a real gem." My voice had gone quite a bit higher throughout this stupid little tirade. Oh yes, I could tell I was being stupid and petty, but there's a difference between knowing and caring.

Del stood over me for a moment, then I heard him settle down on the floor beside me. I stilled and did my best to pretend he didn't exist. "Has something happened to make you unhappy?" he asked after a time. "You've been… your eyes…"

"Crying?" I asked, my voice all watery and cracking, as if to throw evidence at the word. "Oh, that's great—some other totally normal thing for you to wonder at. *They release moisture from their eyes in times of emotion—how strange!* I wonder what I'll do next? Sneeze? Burp? I wonder if rumae ever fart?" Oh boy, I was really far gone now. "A-and yeah, I've been crying, and what do you care about it? Though I get it—maybe it's hard to fathom when I have such a… *happy* little life here. Food, shelter, all of Maslow's bullshit needs. Life's g-great! God, turn off the music, Joanna, I can't fucking take it anymore." One more go-around of the goddamn nocturne would have me drowning in tears.

"You know," Del said, "I don't think it's a trivial thing that you're on board this ship."

I sniffed. "N-no? Could've fooled me."

"There doesn't seem to be much fooling of you at all."

"There's not much *anything* of me at all!" I said, shifting back around to face him. "I just… sit here! I eat, I drink, all the basics. Read. Joanna dresses me up pretty." I coaxed things to grow, then killed them. But I couldn't tell him that was the real reason I was sitting here crying to Chopin, of all things.

We sat quietly for a time. Then I jolted into awareness that, hey, there's a living, breathing person beside me (albeit not a human person), and these days that wasn't an opportunity to squander. Even if he was my captor. Unwilling captor.

So I said, after a few seconds of *should-I-or-shouldn't-I*, "Would you talk a little? Something about yourself? Or a story. Or… anything." The sultan pressing words from Scheherazade. But didn't I deserve them?

"You'd like me to talk."

"Yes, please. It's so quiet here." I missed the sound of conversation, whether that of others around me or people talking right to me: Dad, Molly, Evan, Ray. Joanna, disembodied mole in the walls, barely scratched the itch.

"All right," he said. There was a pause, long enough that I wondered if he understood the assignment. I shifted, stifling in the silence.

"I will tell you about the city where I spend most of my time. *Ohruhn.* It is an old city, a city of... layers. Looking at the city, you could say you see the evidence of all the generations of our people, heaped one over the next like rock strata. Their initial struggles to survive, etched into the stone foundations. Then, eventually, structures that are lighter, more... fanciful. Our people worrying less about their next mouthful of food, daring to think of..." His head cocked as he hunted for the right word. "Aesthetics. Beauty."

"Ohruhn," I said, repeating the name.

"Yes." And in his measured, sometimes halting way, he spun for me an image of a city with ambition, like a sprout bursting forth from a crack in hard mortar—then, strong and sinuous, stretching toward the sky with grasping, greedy tendrils. He spoke of secret chambers at the bottom of the city where untoward sorts conducted business, and sprawling garden platforms in Ohruhn's stratosphere, brimming with life and color. Strong winds sometimes sent gusts of petals raining down to the ground far below. Thoroughfares for flying vehicles wove veinlike through the city, and large high-speed elevators shot up the sides of buildings like rockets launching toward the stars.

"And where do you live?" I asked.

"Our family owns multiple residences throughout Ailopt. But the great house in Ohruhn is our ruling place. That's at the top of the northern part of the city."

"So it's one big house?" I pictured a sort of uprooted White House, jammed atop a skyscraper.

"No," he said. "The great house comprises many separate estate apartments, one for each family member. They stand apart from their surroundings in looks, since all the structures were moved from their original location, what now lies mid-level. An enormous effort that took place generations ago."

"Why the move?"

He rolled his shoulders slightly. "The height reflects our family's might. Our residence must demonstrate our position as rulers. Wealth, power, history. The people must feel that when they see the great house."

It must be strange to live in a symbolic place, especially one made deliberately so. "But... it must be a nice place to live?"

"It is not overly comfortable. A place for work."

"Oh." And so here he was on the *Huivnarrut* and not in Ohruhn. I could understand why he'd prefer his own ship to an over-grand palace. Though the *why-Earth* question still lingered.

"Thank you," I said with a wobbly smile. The crying was behind me now. I could feel the crust of dried tears around my eyes. I must look like a disaster.

He nodded stiffly, and I thought with a little sinking feeling, *duty fulfilled*. Now he'd make his excuses and retreat to his lair and it would be all the same again.

But he didn't make his excuses. Instead he said, "I have prepared something for you."

"What?"

"I prepared something for you," he repeated. "After we spoke yesterday. I wondered if it might get your mind off matters."

"What is it?"

"It is…" He rubbed his jaw with his hand. "Best to show you, I think. If you'd like. You must trust me a little. Special attire is required."

I looked down at my T-shirt and leggings. I'd gone casual today. "Special attire?"

"A—err…" Del paused, head twitching to the side as he waited for his translation tech to serve up the proper word. "A swimsuit?" he finished.

"We're going swimming?"

"You'll have to see," he said, a bit blustery. Okay, I'd have to see. Anything new or novel was welcome—anything to break up the monotony of life on the ship.

"And we're going now?" I asked, wadding up my ball of emotions for later.

"If you'd like."

"Well… sure." He got to his feet, then held out one of his large hands to help me up. I took it, the gritty leather of his palm pressing into my own. He dropped my hand once I'd gotten up. Business as usual.

The fabricator dinged from the other side of the room; I went over and pulled out a rosy two-piece, complete with a ruby red, gauzy, ruffled contraption that I unfurled, confused, until I realized it was a swim cover-up.

"Valentino," Joanna said in a soft voice, all pink—pride, I supposed. I went into the bathroom to change, in my head playing my new favorite game of over-under—whether my new outfit cost over or under a thousand dollars, that is. I was weighing heavily on the side of over.

When I came out, Del had traded his knee-length trousers for ones with a higher hem, no doubt a snappily fabricated Joanna special. Which likely meant that when I'd been changing in there, he'd been doing his own quick-change out here. His legs really were unnervingly muscled, weren't they? Perhaps he was a Thighmaster devotee.

I could see Del taking in my own transformation. The longer tufts of hair around his face fluffed slightly; God knew what that meant.

"Lead the way," I said.

Which he did, out the door, down the hall, and to the elevator.

And this time when he pressed the button for the lower level, the ship responded to its master and down we went.

Chapter Fifteen

THE LOWER LEVEL OF THE SHIP WAS DIMMER THAN UP TOP. IT was warmer, too (I was glad of this, clad in just the swimsuit and cover-up), and there was a low vibration underfoot—all something to do with the ship's power, I guessed. We stepped off the elevator into a sitting room of sorts: thick, furred rugs on the floor, a set of comfy chairs, a shelf of curios lining one wall. The chairs were arranged around a dark, fancy piece of technology shaped like an ottoman for which I had no guesses. A faint, sweet mustiness tinged the air.

Del inclined his head left toward a door at the side, and I followed him through. The room inside was bare and square, though the corners of the room were rounded, rather than coming to a point. No furry rugs here; the floor was a nondescript rubbery material that gave slightly under my feet. Every other surface was slick as glass and emitted a neutral gray light. Del called a few words out in Ziryahshun, and I jumped when the walls responded, taking on a dull violet glow.

He walked to the wall opposite us and pressed a certain

point with his palm. A panel revealed itself, flipping out from the wall to offer us—were those goggles? They were large and intimidating-looking, but there was the back strap and there were the lenses, round as bug eyes.

He took one of the pairs and looked from it to me. "We will need to—" he said with a frown, a white—sharp!—tooth catching at his lip as he thought something over. Then he fiddled with the thin leathery back strap of the goggles until he'd knotted it a few times. Ah. My human head was too small. Not for the first time I wondered what the female half of the rumae species looked like. Were they smaller and daintier than their male counterparts, like so many earthly species? Or larger and more fearsome? I sank into visions of a supersized, feminized version of Del with fabulous hair performing some complex mating ritual that ended with a decapitation, praying mantis-style.

"Here," Del said, handing the goggles to me. The world grew darker when I put them on; they were heavy but comfortable. I looked back at Del and flinched; I swore I could hear liquid sloshing around within the bulky bits at my temples.

"And we're not going swimming?" I asked. I half-expected the room to start filling up with water. Some terrifying alien equivalent of an escape room, perhaps?

He snorted. "Not quite." Not *quite*? "Now take off your… that," he said, flicking a finger at the cover-up. I did so, my arms and legs springing goosebumps. This odd little room was colder than the area outside.

"Now we lay there," Del said, pointing to the center of the rubberized floor, "and… Well, you will see."

"Okay…" This was getting stranger and stranger. He lay down with his arms at his sides, and after a second's hesitation I followed his lead.

"Do not move," he said as soon as I was in the proper position, which shot every one of my nerves into immediate fight-or-flight mode. But I forced myself to stay put, and a moment later, after Del barked another order to the room in Ziryahshun, some sort of glittering gold particulate floated down from the ceiling. I felt like a cake being dusted with powdered sugar by a celestial baker.

"All right, what the fuck?" I asked.

"Roll over," he commanded. Well, why not? There was a moment of awkwardness where we both rolled toward each other and bumped shoulders, then we figured it out, and another dusting of the gold stuff drifted down to coat the back of me. The floor smelled comfortingly of yoga mats.

"Are we seasoned enough?" I asked, and Del gave a growly laugh.

"Yes. Now we get up. You stand there"—he pointed at a particular spot, and I noticed now a faint demarcation line on the floor. "Yes, right there," he said as I moved. "And I will be here," he said, moving a pace away from me.

Then he faced me. "Are you ready?" Speaking of fabulous hair, Del was looking positively radiant with his gold-dust flair. I raised an arm wonderingly; I looked like I'd been touched by King Midas.

"Born ready." I drew a breath; there was a faint sweetness now to the air that I would have sworn hadn't been there moments before. "What are we doing again?"

He shot me a broad grin. "Going kayaking. *Viohr!*"

And then we were there, woods and water melting in around us. Our surroundings were the green vegetation of Earth, none of the violet hues of Tenctah to be seen. A summer's day—birds twittered overhead, a soft wind carried the scent of nature, and I… I was bobbing lightly beside a dock on a wide river, the heat of the sun beating down on my head from above, the cool water below my kayak encircling my lower half.

I loosed a yell, and I heard a chuckle from my right—Del, of course. He looked his usual self now, without the dusting of gold, and he was in a kayak of his own, a big crimson one with no branding, because this was fantasyland. Mine was a gradient that faded from dusky lavender to fuchsia, again no branding.

Fingers trembling, I brought my hands to my face and slowly lifted the goggles. We were still in the room, but the yoga-mat floor beneath my feet was undulating gently, just enough to be barely noticeable. A breeze caressed my cheek, blowing at me from a disguised vent somewhere to the left. I could still feel the battle between the sun and the water on my body and the plastic of the kayak seat against my butt. Mixed messages clashed in my brain—was I standing in a room or floating on a river?

I slipped the goggles back on and rounded on Del, paddling so that the bow rammed his boat. A shiver coursed down my spine when I felt the collision vibrate through me. It was all so *real*—perhaps a shade below real life, but not enough to notice when faced with a picture-perfect landscape.

"You couldn't have warned me? Some sort of heads-up, like,

'Don't freak out, but we're going on a virtual-reality adventure. Keep your arms and legs inside the ride.'"

"Feel free to do whatever you'd like with your appendages," he said, waving his arms around in demonstration. "You said that you were born ready!"

Oh, right, I had said that. Well…

"But—but—" Why was I so pissed off about this? "I've been left alone upstairs, churning through books and twiddling my thumbs, while you were down here in the basement doing… I mean, whatever it is that you do! Are you some sort of video game junkie? Living out your every dream in your magic box? Sex with slave girls, king of the universe…" I'd seen *The Next Generation*. I knew the possibilities. "I've been begging Joanna for access to an air vent so I can smell some real fresh air. While all of this…" I thrust a hand at our surroundings as a breeze, fresh as anything, blew its way toward us. I'd never smelled anything better.

I saw Del's face fall before he looked away down the river, and I knew I'd gone a step too far. Instinct told me he wasn't just puttering around down here playing video games, but that his work was something of consequence. He was Ailopt's heir to the throne, after all.

And he'd said he'd prepared this for me—me specifically. Was that any way to say thank you? My upbringing was suddenly screaming at me.

"That was unkind," I said. "And rude. I-I'm sorry."

He looked back to me, and I couldn't read him. So I waited, as little waves lapped against my boat and the leaves of the trees rustled cheerfully. The strangeness of both sitting down and standing up had faded; maybe I was growing used to it. I could smell soil, sunlight, and the mineral scent of the water. It was beyond convincing, this illusion, and I itched to slide my paddle through the water and move on down the river.

"Rumae and humans are quite similar, I think," he said, breaking his silence at last. "A drive to explore and to conquer. A deep, innate curiosity. A tribal loyalty. But what I did not fully realize is humans' need for social contact. Your species is famed for it, of course—all the texts and research highlight that quality in its extreme degree. As I understand it, isolation is considered one of the harshest punishments in your prisons.

"We rumae… are not like that," he continued, his expression turning pensive. "We enjoy each others' company, but our need for it is not so intense. And I didn't realize… I didn't think…" He looked out over the water. "I thought that what the ship could offer you would be enough. But when we spoke yesterday and you told me of your days here, I realized then more fully the difficulty of your situation.

"And I wished to give you some solace, and you'd expressed your love of nature. Kh—Joanna and I prepared this simulation for you. A scenario with humans to talk to would perhaps be better, but she had a sense you would find that off-putting. So…" He looked back at me. "You should not apologize. My people have a saying. Er—" I could see him struggling with the translation. "'Apologies and deeds make the best bedfellows.' Something like that. You are with us on the ship now; I cannot help that. But maybe this"—he gestured around him—"can be a balm of sorts. A relief."

It was my turn to be quiet for a spell, as nature spun its soft symphony around us of wind, water, birds, and squirrels. His speech had touched me, I'll admit.

"It's very beautiful," I admitted. "How does it work? The smells and the… everything? Like, what's the pixie dust for?"

His red eyes narrowed. "Pixie dust?"

"The gold stuff."

"Ah. It's a type of nanotech that allows for some nerve trickery. The simulation says you should feel heat from the sun, and the nanotech responds accordingly."

"And what's this stuff?" I said, tapping the goggles' large plastic bits at my temple. "There's liquid in there?"

"Yes," he said. "The containers hold scent notes, which get mixed and released in accordance with the simulation."

"Smell-O-Vision," I said wonderingly.

There was a half second's pause. "Right," he said, and I laughed, so obvious was it that he had no clue.

"And the wind effect comes from the built-in fans," I added. "And the goggles do all the rest in terms of the visuals. What about movement?"

"How do you mean?" he asked. He paddled forward a bit. "We can move any way you wish."

"I'm standing. Even though here I'm sitting," I said, pointing down at the kayak. And somehow that wasn't bothering me anymore.

"Ah," he said, understanding me. "There's a small dose of a

gaseous medicine in the air to ease those inconsistencies. It's an aid in your immersion."

"You're drugging me," I clarified.

"Yes…" he said, looking a bit alarmed, like I might start yelling again. "Slightly. *Very* slightly."

"Okay," I said resignedly. I wasn't angry, and maybe that was also down to the drug. Or perhaps it was all such an onslaught of weirdness that I had moved past anger into the realm of acceptance. "And say I were to get out…" I slipped my spray skirt off the kayak and used the dock to boost myself out of the boat and up to standing. "But I don't think I just moved much in real life. But…"

He nodded. "The sim room interprets micro-movements of the body. That effect couples with the medicine in the air, to make you think you're moving more than you are."

I took a cautious step forward with my arms outstretched like I was blind. The wooden planks of the dock creaked pleasantly under my feet. I took another step—still nothing. I looked back at him, confused. "Will I hit the wall eventually?"

His eyes crinkled. "You're standing on an individual patch of reactive floor, which will move you opposite to your intended direction. That is to say, if you walk forward, the floor slides backward."

"It's a treadmill," I said. Really I should have said, *it's magic*. And he'd made all of this for me, I thought, spinning about slowly in a circle. The trees were of a more southern variety than you'd see in Montana—flowering myrtles and orange trees scattered amongst your standard oaks and maples. Their leaves rustled softly in the breeze, here and there revealing brilliant patches of azure sky. A robin hopped on the ground, scouting for worms. Sunbeams cut through the branches overhead, no-see-ums dancing with dust motes in the light.

This beautiful place, all for me. I took one more step forward into the light, reaching out my arms as I reveled in the sunlight on my skin. It lit up the baby hairs on my arms like golden filament.

I heard a slight noise from behind me; Del shifting in his boat. "Do you find it satisfactory?" he asked lightly.

"It's wonderful," I said, turning back around. I blinked; something seemed different in his eyes—relief, I guessed. "Thank you."

He nodded toward the river. "Then would you like to…?"

I couldn't put it into words, but something in that moment felt sacred. A ride in a kayak down a river—I'd done that a thousand times before, but something unformed hung invisible in the air.

"Yes," I said slowly, and wondered at the shakiness in my voice. "L-let's go then! Um… *viohr!*"

He blinked at me, and his mouth broke into another one of those big, toothy smiles. *Rumae dentists must be a thing*, my idiot brain babbled at me. And this guy would star in the Crest commercial. *"Viohr!"* he said with a better accent than my version, plus a lot more excitement than seemed necessary. What had I just gotten myself into?

Oh well, too late to back out now. He used his hand to steady my boat for me as I got back in—and then we were off.

Chapter Sixteen

I WAS NO EXPERT KAYAKER WHEN I WALKED INTO WAKPA Paddling and Ski Center and filled out a job application. I mean, I'd kayaked a couple times at summer camp, but not at any level to write home about.

The tutelage of Ray, my boss, coupled with my subsequent ten thousand or so trips down the Big D these past six years, had gotten me halfway to expert, though. Skiing was all right—I'd done that too as a kid, though breaking my leg on a slope had soured the sport for me—but kayaking was my one true love. There's nothing like the peace of gliding through the water as small paddle strokes let the boat almost move of its own accord, like it's come alive.

That's how it feels in peaceful waters. Then there's whitewater, nature's rollercoaster. The jerk of the boat against rocks unseen or unavoidable, the ledges that make your stomach drop, the spray of frigid water on your face—I love all that as well, in a different way. There's no comparing the two.

"Kayaking's a funny sort of sport," I remembered Ray saying

when he was teaching me. He's on the shorter side, with a stocky build and a permanent tan from all the time he spends outside. He revealed to me once that he used to weigh four hundred pounds, most of which he'd shed when he, in his words, left his long-time mistress of fast food for the sweeter embrace of time spent outdoors. He'd met his wife along the way—I mean this both figuratively and literally, since they'd met each other while hiking alongside the Big D—and they eventually opened the shop. The rest was history.

"The thing with a lot of sports," Ray said to me as we paddled side by side down the river, "is that you get better at them, and they get a bit less treacherous. Take rock climbing, for example. You're cautious when you start, then around the one-to-three year mark you gain some experience and take some risks—that's the most perilous point of a rock climber's career. But after that you come to know your limits and the chance of death levels out.

"But kayaking, especially if you like rapids, the better you get at it the easier it is to die. You want a bigger challenge, you think you can handle such-and-such river, and oops, actually no. You roll and get caught under the boat, you hit your head, you get hypothermia… there are all manner of ways you can end up dying. Happens all the time. So you can't get cocky. Nature's great at killing people."

He'd said all this to me, then cracked a smile and slapped the side of his boat. "It's fun though, huh?"

Now as Del and I set out down the river, whatever reservations I'd had about simulated kayaking were slipping away.

The wizardry of the nanobots let me feel the paddle in my hands, even though I held nothing but empty air. I could feel the boat bobbing gently on the river beneath me, though my own two feet remained rooted to the floor. Sure, it wasn't real—but that was something I had to keep reminding myself.

Del looked, well… not exactly *ridiculous* in his red kayak, but the effect was amusing; his upper body was so large and hulking that he looked about ready to capsize the poor boat. Weight limits didn't seem to be a thing in this simulation. I briefly tried to envision what model I would have suggested to him if he'd have strolled into our store and asked for recommendations, only to come up blank.

"Lead the way," he said, so I pulled ahead and quickened the pace a bit.

"You good with this?" I called, looking back over my shoulder. His form wasn't incredible, but what could you expect from a beginner?

"Of course." He looked miffed that I'd dare suggest he wasn't. Oh, was that how it was going to be? Fun. I upped my speed again and laughed when I heard a load of messy splashing from behind me.

We continued on that way for a while, me slipping through the water cool, calm, collected, while he tried to brute-force it. At last I took pity on him and let him catch up.

"You're not holding the paddle right." He bristled—His Liege clearly wasn't used to hearing critique. "Well, you're not!" I said, sitting tall and lifting my chin in challenge. "There's a right way and a wrong way, and you're doing it wrong!"

He glowered at me, and I glowered right back. "What do you suggest?" he grumbled, once our staring contest wore thin.

Ah-hah—victory. "Well," I said, trying to keep the gloat from my voice, "the longer edge of your paddle blades should be on top, and… Oh, you have them flipped around, too. The scooped side of the blade should face you. Right, that's better. And your grip is too tight. Now we'll do a basic forward stroke…"

I took him through a mini lesson. I've subbed for the instructors at the shop on occasion, so I have a practiced spiel. It was a good day for a beginner's lesson—placid water, not much wind.

Del was an apt pupil, once he got over being told what to do. When I was satisfied that he had a decent grasp of how to move the boat, we continued down the river. I let him take the lead this time, so I could watch and call out pointers.

It also happened to be a very interesting view. I found my eyes straying from Del's paddling technique up to his back, his arms, the bushy tangle of hair falling wild from his head down over his shoulders. All of this from a pure appreciation of physicality, of course, like how you can't help but admire the rippling musculature of Budweiser's Clydesdale horses.

It was getting hot out here in the sun. I paddled back up to join him.

"Huh-lowuh," he said as I drew up alongside him.

"Hey there," I said. "Um, *grr… grrup…*"

"*Grrup dih,*" he prompted.

"Right—*grrup dih.* It looks like the river's forking up ahead. Did you want to go left or right?"

He cupped the fingers of one hand together, before spreading his fingers wide, palm up. Then he waited for me to speak.

"Oh," I said. "Yes, I see." I did not see. "Okay then."

He seemed to remember that he wasn't speaking with a fellow rumae. "Ah. It means, er, *the choice lies with the lady*. You see, because—" And he made the same motion again, slowly and with more purpose.

"Yes, obviously," I said. Rumae. "Well, if it's up to me, then I suppose…" The right-hand fork was wider than the left, and the trees on either bank overhung the river to nearly form a canopy. Pretty, and no doubt spectacular in falltime—but something about the winding curve of the narrower fork was calling my name. "That way," I said, swinging toward the left. From the corner of my eye, I could have sworn that Del had just leaned forward in his seat by a hair. I glanced at him, and he looked a bit—bigger? Fluffier? Like a slightly startled cat, though his eyes held a focused excitement. Something told me I'd picked the choice he'd been hoping for. Oh boy, what had I just roped myself into?

We continued down the river a few more minutes. The once-calm water was growing faster and choppier, and the river ahead was pockmarked with boulders. All signs pointed to whitewater.

"This might be too much for your skill level," I called to Del. *Might be* was an understatement to save his pride—he didn't even know how to Eskimo roll. I cast a glance back over my shoulder; his boat was rocking back and forth alarmingly, but somehow every time capsizing seemed imminent he managed to right it. He was either lucky beyond belief or he'd done something like this before.

"Worry for yourself, not me!" he shouted back over the rush of the water when he caught me looking. "It's merely a simulation!" The timber of his voice had deepened, every muscle intent, and he was grinning. Daredevil, huh?

I fought to keep the rocks at bay, the surging currents batting my boat this way and that. The Big D this was not. My boat bounced and juddered against hidden river rocks, the freezing spray stealing my breath away. It was ludicrous to be doing all this in a bikini and no helmet—but this was just a simulation, I reminded myself, as I wrestled with a current that threatened to dash me against a craggy boulder fast approaching. Steer left… even more left… oh God, I was really going to hit it…

I cleared the boulder with an inch to spare, the water swelled beneath me and rocketed me forward, everything became a roar in my ears, and I was soaring down a waterfall.

Chapter Seventeen

I WAS SCREAMING. DIMLY, I HEARD A THUNDEROUS CRY JOIN IN: Del. The slap as my boat hit the surface and the icy embrace of the water came at me like a one-two punch, and when the boat bounced back up I screamed again, just to prove I was alive.

Somehow I hadn't rolled, and the water was buffeting me toward calmer currents—a good thing, because I'd lost my grip on the paddle as I fell. Weariness was already winning out over adrenaline, accompanied by bone-chilling numbness. I could only draw breath in sharp little sips; *hypothermia*, a little voice in my head whispered before I quashed it. This wasn't real. *This wasn't real.*

"It's not real," Del's deep voice said from behind me. I turned; he was looking positively electrified, though his expression went a bit strained when he looked my way. Trust the guy with fur to not understand that his hairless, bikini-clad companion might take issue with plunging down a waterfall into glacial river water. He looked only slightly worse for wear, most of the water beading off his fur.

"I-I know it's not r-real," I whispered through chattering teeth. "Jesus f-fucking Christ." This I directed more toward the world at large than at him. The waterfall loomed behind him… Had we really just fallen down *that*? The drop had to be at least thirty feet.

When I looked back to Del, he looked yet more uncomfortable. Then his eyes did that concealed downward flick any large-chested girl knows well, and through the cold I had a jolting realization that all was not right down under.

"Oh!" Wheeling away from him, I looked down to find that during the fall my right breast had managed a complete escape from my bikini top; the left cup was hanging on by prayer alone. I stuffed myself back together again, pulled on a smile to cover my mortification, then turned around.

"A heads-up next t-time would be n-nice." I still couldn't stop shivering.

As he nodded, I could have sworn some glimmer in his eyes laughed at me. "Of course. Next time I will be sure to let you know."

"Would you m-mind getting me to shore?" Surely he and his muscles could handle that.

Most people would have jerry-rigged a way to rope the boats together, but instead Del came up alongside me and seized hold of my boat with one arm. Then he grabbed his paddle with his other arm, and with strong, deep strokes he started towing me to shore. My skin burned as the day's heat and the warm sun began to beat the cold out of me.

We reached land at last—not a dock, but a small grassy clearing complete with a circle of cinder blocks to form a firepit. To the side was a ramshackle hutch stacked full of firewood. Del clambered ashore first, then tugged me in. I was grateful for the steady hand he offered me as I rose from the boat, shaky and bedraggled, and stepped onto the grass.

While I flopped to a seat on the ground, Del busied himself starting a fire. His movements as he arranged the logs and scouted the ground for kindling had the ease of someone who'd done this before. As for starting the fire itself, it turned out that the lumpy woven sash he wore from shoulder to hip wasn't just the strange fashion statement I'd taken it to be, but concealed tools; from a hidden inner pocket he fished out a shiny black bauble that revealed itself to be a lighter, and from another a tiny bottle of some dark, oily substance that he dripped onto the logs as a firestarter. Soon enough, the merry crackle of flames filled our little clearing. Del gave the fire a sort of satisfied frown—princely even here, as if he were commanding the fire to keep burning. Then he sat down on the ground a few feet from me, and a silence stretched between us. He was waiting, I think, for me to berate him.

It was the scariest thing I'd ever done, but also the coolest thing I'd ever done. That he had put together this entire place for me—that was somehow warming me almost as much as the campfire currently drying my damp hair into frizzing golden waves. And now I found it hard to look at him for some reason.

I shifted my gaze instead to the waterfall behind us. "I can't believe we actually made it down that thing."

From the corner of my eye I saw him give me a look. "Of course we did."

It was just the sort of haughty, Del-ish thing he would say. "What do you mean, 'of course we did?'" I said, turning to face him. Banter—that was a safer territory than whatever nebulous place my thoughts had strayed to a moment ago. "I ran you through a lesson I normally give to all the peewees. *I've* never gone down anything like that"—I waved a hand at the veritable Niagara Falls behind us—"so I have no idea how *you* made it down in one piece. You're like a… a kayaking prodigy."

He chuckled quietly. "But remember, it's not real."

"No, I understand that," I said. "But—"

"This simulation is crafted for entertainment," he said, interrupting me. "To bring the user to a sensational brink—that is entertainment. Any more and the experience would become too frightening. So…"

My jaw dropped as I realized what he was saying. "We're playing on easy mode."

"Yes," he said. "An apt way of putting it. But… thank you for your belief in my kayaking abilities."

It should have been obvious, but I'd been so swept up in the reality of the moment. "What things do *you* normally like to do in here?" I asked, skimming a hand over the top of the grass, the blades tickling my palm. "In this room."

"Me?" he asked, looking taken aback. Oh—was that maybe a gauche question? Perhaps it was like asking someone to list their favorite porn categories.

I gave a tinkly little laugh to keep the conversation moving.

"I mean, I can think of so many things I'd do in here. I'd play the role of Elizabeth in *Pride and Prejudice*—that's a book," I explained. "Or I'd fly over the Grand Canyon—that's a place way south of here. Or I'd go to space."

Or I'd see Mom again, said an unbidden voice in my head softly. I shivered. Whenever Molly and I had watched a holodeck episode of *Star Trek*, I'd always thought the technology seemed too tempting for mankind. That small voice, whispering from some dark corner of my psyche, said my suspicions were merited.

"I can show you space," Del said, leaning forward. "Easily. Would you like to see?"

Alarm bells clamored in my head; he really *could* take me to space. "Not… not actually, right? You mean here in the room?"

He nodded. "Right here."

"Then yes," I said. "But wait a moment." Because the nature all around us was rooting me to the ground.

So we waited, while the water gurgled and the wind soughed. I breathed in the smoke, remembering other times around the campfire—s'mores when I was a kid, terrible beer when I was in high school. Looking to the trees, I let my eyes go unfocused until the forest was a soft, verdant blur. Eventually Del lay back on the grass, stretching long—not in a way that said *hurry up*, but the very opposite. *Take your time.* And something within me that had long been huddled in on itself began to uncurl.

Some time later I returned to myself, refocusing my gaze. All moments must come to a close.

I drew in one last breath, tasting the sweet interplay of smoke and greenery. "All right. I'm ready now."

With a quiet word from Del the world around us blinked out. Free-floating, bodiless, I found myself gliding through a yin-yang landscape: to the left a titanic, burning sun that gobbled up half my vision, to the right the cold black void of space. Stars pricked the darkness. Del's soft breathing came from my right somewhere; save for that, the silence was absolute.

"Our sun," he said softly after a moment. "*Uvoren*. And now…"

Two invisible spirits, we sped in tandem away from Uvoren's terrible, fiery mass. A shriveled, blackened planet came and went, followed by another wreathed in misty teal vapors, followed by another of swirling gray gases.

And then a bulbous nebula sprawled before us, awash in shades of ochre and turquoise. Offshoot tendrils ballooned outward like a god's outstretched fingers. We dove toward the cloudy mass, the stars at the corners of my vision stretching into brilliant, dizzying streamers of light. A cluster of asteroids hurtled past; how many million (billion?) miles were we traveling per minute? The nebula's colors dimmed as we approached, then faded altogether. We were inside it now.

A planet emerged from the darkness, swelling from a tiny pixel dot to a colossal globe. The surface was a clash of rich blue water and dark reddish earth, veiled by violet-tinged clouds. A moon—no, two moons!—floated alongside the planet.

And from the side of the planet cloaked in nighttime shadows, the golden light of civilization shone out: here the sparse glow of rural land, there the bright radiance of cities. We drew a little closer, and now I could see that the clouds above the surface glinted every so often with silver: satellites and spaceships.

This was Tenctah; it had to be. I'd never seen anything more beautiful. I exhaled a ragged breath.

"Corinne?" Del sounded worried. I felt a soft movement of air; he'd moved closer to me in the room. "You… You're not crying again, are you?"

"No. No, I mean, yes. A-a little." It was true that I'd shed a few tears; how couldn't you? Just one or two. They pooled against my cheek under the goggles. "It's so beautiful. I didn't expect it to be so beautiful."

"I feel the same way as you," he said, "every time I come or go. Here, I'll show you Ailopt." There was a swell of pride in his voice.

We glided leftward, soaring high above a churning ocean, then an expansive flatland of lighter red. We were moving towards the side of the planet in nighttime, where the city lights glittered.

"Here," he said after a minute, and we came to a halt. The land below was studded with golden glowing cities, a lot of them.

"All of this?" I asked.

"All of this…" he said, then spoke a word, and the land lit up with a soft silver to denote the territory and borders of his country. Middle-school geography would have been much more impactful with a sim room, I mused.

Ailopt was a massive country with a muddied squiggle of borders that spoke of interesting relationships with its neighbors. Mountain ranges formed rocky wrinkles in the east and southwest, and flatter plains spread across the southeast. A large lake cut into the northern territory. And everywhere the electric light of life beat back the night.

"How many people—rumae—live in Ailopt?" I asked softly, bracing myself.

I hadn't braced myself enough. "Two billion," he said, and I drew a sharp breath. "And more on our various colonies. We've terraformed Eelagov—that is one of Tenctah's moons—and there are about one hundred million living there now. All those of Ailoptian citizenship… perhaps two and a half billion, all told."

"Tell me you didn't come to Earth to colonize it," I said. I'd wondered, of course—who wouldn't? But only now, under this false cover of darkness and with Ailopt's might spread plainly before me, had I summoned the courage to ask him at last.

"No," his voice said gravely from beside me. "It's a… a happenstance that I am here."

"You swear?" I asked. I heard a murmur, and Ailopt blinked out, replaced by the small, plain interior of the sim room.

Disorientation crashed over me, and I staggered backwards as the room swung about, like I was drunk. His hand caught my shoulder, and I felt his other hand on my waist as he lowered me gently to a seated position on the ground. I threw off the goggles and hung my head between my legs, breathing fast.

"That can happen sometimes," he said. "Especially to those

not accustomed to such simulations. I should have thought to warn you."

"Why'd you end it?" I wiped the sweat from my forehead; there was a lot I would give for the comfort of a warm bath right now. The room was still spinning. I closed my eyes.

"Because you asked me to swear it. That I haven't come to Earth for… colonization purposes."

"It's more just an expression," I said, even though I hadn't meant it that way, not really.

"A serious question deserves a serious response. I would have you look at me, instead of answering you unseen."

Oh. I forgot about his princeliness sometimes. "All right, then."

I lifted my head from between my legs and found Del sitting on the floor opposite me, looking concerned. That seemed to be the theme of the day.

"I'm really okay," I said, offering him a weak smile. "Hardly dizzy at all now." Lies—we Kaminskis just don't like to admit weakness as a general rule, like an animal hides an illness.

He looked pleased at that, then his expression grew serious. "I swear this to you: my coming to Earth has nothing to do with colonization."

"What about the killing of humans, the enslavement of humans, anything like that?"

"None of it. I am simply… here. Visiting. Temporarily. I hope to pass on from your planet without disturbing anyone else from Earth."

"That's a good plan," I said with a bit more strength. The

room was starting to settle again. "Lord knows you've disturbed me enough. I'm kidding! I'm kidding," I added at his look of chagrin. "I really should say… thank you. Not for bringing me to the ship, I mean, but for this." I motioned around us at the sim room. "It was… I've never seen anything like it. Not even close. Thank you."

"You could use it again soon, if you'd like." His red eyes held my own, unwavering. "We could. There's the other fork in the river."

I'd forgotten about that. I gave him a slim smile. "You're just looking for some free kayaking lessons. And I don't work for free."

He scoffed. "What need for lessons? I am, as you say, a kayaking prodigy."

"Right," I said dryly. "Though your terrible technique says otherwise."

"I won't stand to be so insulted on my own ship."

"Time to get good, then." He looked at me with mock fury, and I looked right on back narrowly. This was fun.

"The lady drives a hard bargain," he said after the requisite amount of seconds to preserve his male ego. "I will submit to your lesson."

"For a price. Like I said, I don't work for free."

"Name your price," he said, with a slight incline of his head.

In that moment, I think the both of us felt what I really wanted shimmering unspoken in the air. But it would have ruined the play-fighting to say it, and saying it would have been useless besides. This was my life now.

"Show me something you like to do," I said, scrambling for an answer. "Kayaking's my thing. You must have a thing."

"A thing."

"You know, a hobby." For a second he looked at me so blankly that I was worried he didn't actually have anything to show me. Maybe being princely was all he had time to do.

But then he nodded briskly. "There is something I can show you. Tomorrow, perhaps. Though it's rather… fearsome." His eyes shone with challenge.

Oh dear. Well, I guess I'd swum into the deep end voluntarily, so now I had to deal with the consequences. "Fine."

"Then it's a deal?"

My stomach did a little flip. Lord help me—how had this gotten switched around to where I was the one doing the agreeing? "Deal."

Chapter Eighteen

COMETS AND SUNS AND STARS—MY DREAMS TOOK ME BACK INTO the cosmos that night. There before me was the beckoning wonder of Tenctah, glittering like a jewel in the velvet darkness of space. Then, in the off-kilter way of dreams, I was back on Earth in the sun-drenched summertime—and Del a welcome presence beside me. We were laughing, joking together. And the sun had grown low, the sky awash with fiery crimson and yellow—

A whisper: *"Corinne."*

The both of us on the river now, Del on his boat, his back to me. The red light of the sun set the definition of his body in sharp, shadowed relief. He was shocking to look at—primal. I couldn't look away.

"Corinne. Wake up."

I gasped awake, my skin prickling with heat. The walls of my room were red as my dream, a thick, bloody red, and they squirmed with worry.

"What's wrong?" I asked. "What time is it?" Unnervingly, I'd never heard Joanna whisper before.

"My deepest apologies—it's three in the morning. I... the master... I think he's in need of some assistance."

"Assistance?"

"That's right. Just to be sure, I think you'd better check on him."

Check on him? I'd never heard her sound so hesitant before.

But why not? "Okay," I said, swinging my legs out of bed with a groan. My head ached like I'd—well, like I'd just been woken up at three in the morning. I wrapped myself up in my fuzzy bathrobe, put on my slippers, then gave Midge a scritch on the head. She was out cold and giving breathy little snores.

"All right," I said. "Where am I going?"

"Downstairs, to the master's quarters."

So with a tired nod I headed out of my room toward the elevator. The halls of the ship were eerier at night, even though they were lit the same as ever. I walked with a floaty feeling of unreality, as if I were still half-dreaming.

The elevator responded to my touch instantly; seconds later I was in the lower level. The room before me was even dimmer than before, the corners of the room cloaked in shadows. I looked around; there was the door to the left that opened into the sim room and doors at the far end of the room and to the right that led to parts unknown. Del was nowhere to be seen.

I wrinkled my nose; the air was thick with an unpleasant sweetness. Something about the odor was faintly familiar. *Recently* familiar. Where had I smelled it before?

"What's that smell?" I asked Joanna quietly as I stepped out of the elevator.

"Later," she said. "He's in the sim room. Just... just poke your head in and see if he's all right?"

The sim room—that jogged my memory. Hadn't I caught a whiff of this same smell right before we'd gone "kayaking"?

But hang on now. I might still feel half-asleep, but I was awake enough to have a question or two. "Can't you see in the room?" I asked, frowning.

"Unfortunately, no." She sounded deeply uncomfortable.

"Why?"

"He... he's temporarily restricted my permissions on this level. I'm not allowed inside."

Curiouser and curiouser. But she wanted *me* to go inside, with a likely result of him biting my head off. In a figurative sense, one hoped. I sidled closer to the door with some amount of trepidation.

"Why did he restrict your access? Is that something he does often? God, that smell!" Another wave of it had just hit me.

"Corinne, could you *please* just check on him first?"

And she sounded so nervous that that was fine by me. I strode to the door and pushed the button.

That same thick smell spilled out as the door rolled open. Tears pricked my eyes.

"God!" I reeled back from the door. What *was* that? I still hadn't seen into the room.

"What is it?" cried Joanna.

I pressed my palms to my tearing eyes. "You can't smell that?" But of course she didn't have a nose. "It's sweet. Kind of... musty?"

"Oh," she said, in a tone that meant, *oh no*. "Best put something over your mouth and nose. Take shallow breaths."

Nodding, I untied my bathrobe and slipped the collar of my nightshirt up over my nose. Right, now to see to Del. I turned back to the door and went in.

And there he was in the middle of the room, slumped in a heap on the ground. He had the goggles on, and his body glinted with the gold shimmer of the nanotech. The room's rubbery floor pulsed beneath him, as if some desperate creature were trapped under the floor, attempting to claw its way out. And still Del did not move, as the floor beneath him shuddered and quaked.

A disembodied man's voice spoke, a taunting tone to his words. All in Ziryahshun, though, so who was to say for sure?

"How do I turn it off?" I asked Joanna, then realized the door had slid shut automatically behind me. Annoyed, I jabbed at the button to open it and repeated my question out into the other room.

"Is he all right?" she asked, frantic.

Time to get it together, Joanna. "Not sure. Tell me how to turn the room off."

"Tell it, *zahm haeyuptirr*." At least that's what I thought she'd said, and when I did my best interpretation the floor slowed, then settled.

I rushed over to him. He was breathing, I saw straightaway, his broad chest rising and falling with the slow, even rhythm of deep sleep. Sleeping, even when the floor beneath him had been moving like that? And even in sleep he looked… not at ease, sort of unwell. Smaller than the Del I knew, like he'd shrunken in on himself.

I slipped off his goggles; yes, his eyes were closed. I touched his arm, gave him a little shake. Nothing.

"Drugged," I murmured, shaking his arm again. And now he responded, pulling me down to wrap himself around me. One arm tugged me inward to his chest, the other draped over me, deadweight, pinning me down.

Joanna had said to take shallow breaths; I stopped breathing entirely. Well, what are you supposed to do when a large alien decides to spoon you in his sleep? And he *was* still sleeping, I could tell. His body was a warm, snug, motionless cave around me. Or… I jerked forward an inch, startled, which only caused him to draw me in tighter, like I was stuck in a Chinese finger trap. Let's just say that, contrary to initial observation, the rise and fall of his chest wasn't the only part of him that was moving.

I took stock of the situation. Del was obviously under the influence of some soporific—likely the gaseous drug he'd mentioned to me earlier, here present in much larger quantities. That accounted for the smell, though it was starting to dissipate now that I'd turned the room off. And what was the purpose of the drug again? To let the user become more immersed in the experience—that's how I remembered him explaining it.

What sort of perverted sexcapades had Del been simulating when the tech that dispensed the gas had gone haywire? That was the likeliest explanation for how he'd come to be lying on the ground, dead to the world, and in this sort of—eager state. No way to know how long he'd been like this or when he'd come out of it, but at least he didn't seem to be under any sort of serious distress. In fact he now seemed quite—I scooched my ass forward another inch—*quite happy*. Thank goodness the door had slid shut again; the last thing I wanted was Joanna catching sight of this.

And Lord help me, in that rare moment away from Joanna's ever-watchful presence, I took a second. Del and I had shared odd touches here and there, but nothing prolonged. Midge and I cuddled, sure, but at the end of the day she was still a dog. It had taken an alien abduction to give me a deeper understanding of the parts of me that made me human—and a need for touch was one of those things, I realized now, as I just… stayed there, in his arms. The heat of his body against me, the soft brush of his ruddy fur… And his smell was all around me—a deep, musky, male scent. I relaxed into him…

"Corinne?" Joanna's tense voice filtered through the door, and I sucked in a breath; I'd nearly fallen asleep. Or had actually fallen asleep. Which side of the looking glass was I on right now, anyway? At three in the morning, any reality can skew a bit cuckoo.

"Corinne?" she called again. "Everything all right?"

"Um…" All I could think of was how Del had shifted forward again, the long, hard length of him pressed against my thigh.

"You're very blessed," I whispered to him as I dropped lower to the ground and began a complicated wriggling maneuver to escape. At last I freed myself and surged to my feet in triumph, at which Del's brow furrowed and he rolled over onto his other side with a frustrated growl.

I opened the door and was confronted by a kaleidoscope. It pulsated wildly at me. *"What's going on in there?"* demanded Joanna.

I thanked my lucky stars I'd worked retail long enough to have full control over my facial features. "He's fine," I said, stepping back into the main room. "He just needs to sleep it off. But you need to calm down."

"What took you so long?"

"I was checking his breathing and his pulse."

"For nine minutes?"

God, had it been that long? "I, um, also turned him onto his side. Thought maybe he'd vomit and choke on it. And that took a while because he's so big."

Big and long, volunteered a psychotic part of my brain. *Shut up. SHUT. UP.*

Her technicolor shards went softer at the edges. "Oh. Thank you."

"You're welcome."

"Best not to speak of this with him, I think." Interesting— wasn't Joanna's allegiance to Del sacrosanct? How did keeping secrets fit into that relationship?

"Right…" I jerked my chin towards the sim room. "So what was going on in there?" I let a smile play over my lips.

"That's best kept between myself and the master."

"You said check on him first, then we'd talk."

"I…"

"But you didn't mean it," I finished for her when she said no more. Her silence was all the confirmation I needed.

My eyes roved around the room. It looked exactly the same

as it had before, but the witching hour lent it a surreal quality.

"Well, crisis averted!" Joanna said brightly. "My deepest thanks—really." Her meaning couldn't have been more obvious. *Let's sweep this under the rug, and now it's time for you to go.*

"Mm-hm," I said, side-stepping a lounge chair to move closer to the strange, technological ottoman in the center of the room. There was a little switch on one side; ooh, how I yearned to push it. Or what about the other doors here? Where did they lead?

"It's getting late," she said.

I might never get another opportunity like this, with Del fast asleep and Joanna unable to tattle on me, lest Del find out about tonight's events. Whether she liked it or not, it was snooping time.

"What are you doing?" she hissed at me with bright white frustration as I drew closer to the ottoman.

"What is this?" I asked.

"Don't... Stop touching that!"

"What is it?"

She made a little strangled noise as I glided a finger gently over the button on the side. "It's a... Well, there's nothing quite like it on Earth! A bit like a TV or a smartphone. Corinne, you really shouldn't touch the master's things without his permission."

Too late; I'd already pushed the button. I took a quick step back as the interlocked metal top of the ottoman unfurled and retracted, revealing a glowing swirl of green and white vapor. It was like a techy witch's cauldron.

The cauldron jabbered something in a robotic tone. It sounded like a question.

"Corinne—"

"*Viohr.*"

The vapor knit together into lines of light. It was a simulation of some sort: a topographic map of a rocky-looking surface, its face scarred with fissures. A ghostly white shape hared between the rifts, some sort of pod-like vehicle. It traveled from south to north, the pod's position resetting every time it reached a jagged, crooked angle in the rift. I bent closer as the room's walls sparkled with copper barbs—Joanna's equivalent of throwing up her hands in frustration, I figured.

"Okay, okay," I said after a moment's more study, then turned my gaze to the door opposite me. More bursts of copper around me—all right, I was definitely going in. Joanna groused as I crossed the room (*wholly inappropriate, invasion of privacy,* and so on and so forth) which only made me the more certain that—I pushed the button with an internal prayer—yes, this door slid open easily for me, almost eagerly.

Joanna maintained her silence, seething and neon.

Shadows shrouded the space inside; one orb light flicked on overhead as I passed through the door. Joanna's fractals slunk in with me, keeping to the corners and the wall seams.

The room was not large, but even so, it was far too big a space for what it contained: a large but unassuming bed with plain sheets and a thin gray blanket folded in a square at the foot; a fabricator in the wall; a simple desk and chair, crafted from dark wood. That was it. There wasn't even a rug.

This was how the heir to the throne of a populace of two and half billion lived? It was spartan, almost ascetic. Where were the gilt doodads, the kingly furnishings? "This is Del's bedroom?" I asked, turning. "But—"

And now I saw the familiar dark screen, tucked in the corner behind me. It was a mirror like my own, but its surface was gouged with—with… I drifted nearer.

He had raked the mirror's surface with his claws, had carved grooves in it that cut all the way through to the magical tech within. Most of the damage was towards the top, where he… where his head might be in the reflection. The mirror's exposed innards winked at me, gleaming, from within.

I crept back through into the main room. Everything was very, very quiet, my companion saying not a word—not even when I came to the final door. I pushed the button.

This door, too, opened to darkness, but when I crossed the threshold this time no light blinked on. The dim light from the room behind me was no help in beating back the darkness; a few steps in I was surrounded by inky shadows.

I stopped, waiting for my eyes to adjust. I had a sense of a large, uneven, crooked kind of space. The air in here was cold, much colder than the main room, and I pulled my bathrobe close. Taking a step forward, I stumbled a little; there was debris underfoot. And Joanna, now a furious icy blue, was gliding inside and filling the walls, but… My eyes widened.

Some great force had torn the walls asunder, ripping them apart so that Joanna seemed to peer at me through a cracked mirror. A black, caulk-like glop stitched together the uneven seams. Joanna's blue bathed the room in an eerie light, and I saw now that this was the heir apparent's real bedroom—or what was left of it.

It looked like a bomb had gone off. Furniture in splinters, machinery smashed to smithereens, decorations shredded. One piece of a mattress lay at the far side of the room, the other piece nearer to me; it had been ripped cleanly in two. Foamy stuffing from within spilled out to coat the floor like snow. Overhead the ceiling had been mostly torn off, revealing the ship's inner skeletal workings: pipes, cords, wires, chips, beams. A few of the larger gaping pockets revealed glimpses of other rooms in the level above. All those doors I had tried to open in my first few days here, thinking it was because they offered me possible escape… And maybe that was true of some of them, but how many others hid this absolute ruin?

"What did this?" I asked her. Because Del had done the damage to the mirror in the other room, that was clear enough, but this…

She didn't answer me.

"An attack," I said slowly. "Something like that."

A shiver rippled through her, but still she said nothing.

"Or a crash. An accident. Did it happen here, on Earth? Or somewhere else, and then you came here to do the repairs?" Was this where Del was always disappearing to? Repairing the ship so he could make the trip back to Tenctah…

"I can't tell y—"

"Yes, you can!" I said sharply, feeling something within me fracture. "I'm one half of this ship's occupants!"

Her next words, when they came at last, were utterly stiff and proper. "My apologies, but that is the master's private matter."

There was a fist-sized piece of rubble at my feet; I picked it up and heaved it at her. It lodged in the wall with a crunching sound, and the smoothness of her fractals around the debris shattered into glitching primary colors. She recoiled.

"Corinne, I can't—"

"Fine!" I was so angry I could barely speak. "I get it. But next time you want to wake me up in the middle of the night to check on your precious master, see if I do it."

Then I stomped off, and if she trailed me back to my suite, well, who was to know? I didn't look back to check.

Chapter Nineteen

IT WOULD HAVE BEEN NICE TO SLEEP IN, BUT I SHUDDERED awake just a few hours later. The walls were an unmarred dusty mauve, with just the faintest orange shadow in the corners.

I sat up and brought my knees in to my chest. "Let me see outside," I said, and instantly I was surrounded by my mountains. Their snowy peaks were pink with alpenglow. I breathed in, almost able to smell the scene from memory: coldness, faintly sweet, laced with pine.

I looked out over the mountains for a long, long time, tracing their stark silhouettes with my eyes. I thought of spats I'd had with Molly before, for the pettiest of reasons, it always seemed afterwards. And I thought of the desolation of that room below, how cold it had been.

Rising from the bed, I walked to the wall. I laid my palm against it gently; despite being a screen, it was quite cool to the touch. Then I leaned my forehead against the wall. This close up, the projection lost its reality—not pixelated, exactly, but a bit blurry, sort of stretched. If this were real glass I should be able to see my reflection, but it wasn't there.

"I'm sorry I threw that at you," I said at last, turning away. The words were raw and sour in my mouth in that post-fight way. I didn't mean them. Yet the words had to be said, to move on.

Home isn't so far away. A mile. Less, even. Remember that.

Joanna faded in a little, just ghostly translucent lines here and there. "Corinne, I'm on your side, as much as I can be. There are limitations…"

"I understand. It's got to be difficult."

"It is…" But though her form was now a bit more solid, she still looked wan, listless. For an AI who was built to serve, what I needed was a peace offering in her language.

I pulled on a happier face. "Today I was thinking I might try that soil test kit you made me."

She brightened, literally. "Oh, really? Well, that sounds fun."

"And I think some rubber gloves would be useful—could you make me some? And maybe some paper towels…" I'd decided to try my hand at cleaning up the hothouse, and I rattled off a few more requests, each one bringing back more of her color than the last.

She hummed to herself as she got to work with the fabricator, while I got dressed and pondered how wrong it was to take candy from a baby. When it was time to go, I left with my new supply of blue nitrile gloves, as well as a pair of new gardening gloves, the paper towels, a kneeling pad, a bamboo trellis, a tarp, a trowel with a nicer grip, a weighty metal tumbler, and a big tote bag with an English-rose pattern to lug my haul. The tumbler had a screw-on lid, which I was happy to see looked very sturdy and air-tight.

"Won't it be fascinating if you actually find something wrong with the soil you can, well, *diagnose?*" Joanna asked as we—I—walked. There was that jaunty Britishness I'd come to know so well.

"I can't wait," I said, still at odds with myself.

It had been a few years since I'd done any sort of in-depth soil analysis, so I'd made sure to read the test kit instructions over at least a half dozen times just to be sure I had the process correct. First came the soil extraction, then the demineralized water, then a milliliter of the buffer solution…

Now, with bated breath, I added two drops of indicator to the beaker in front of me and swirled the solution around. The liquid bloomed wine red, indicating calcium and magnesium. All was going to plan. The next step was to add the EDTA, swirling again after each drop. The red liquid in the beaker grew purpler, edging towards blue. Perhaps one more drop? Yes, there it was: a true, blue hue. And then to use all that information with my handy-dandy formula… A few chicken-scratch calculations in the margins of the test-kit instructions uncovered definitively that yes, there were healthy levels of calcium and magnesium in the hothouse soil.

I scowled at the beaker and pushed it aside to join the other plethora of vessels, spoons, and pH strips that surrounded me on the floor of the gazebo. By all indications the hothouse soil was normal, and normal meant boring. What was causing my monster plants? It had to be some element native to Tenctah and absent on Earth.

Midge gave a bored groan from the other side of the gazebo, where she'd flopped down for a nap while I did my science. She was giving me side-eye; it was time to go.

"Some lab partner you are," I grumbled at her as I dumped all the lab equipment back into its box, then pushed that under the gazebo seat to join the wilted remains of my vegetables. This space was fast becoming a repository of all things Joanna couldn't be allowed to know.

"I want to try nitrate of potash," I told Joanna when I rejoined her at the wall a minute later.

"Really?" She sounded truly surprised. "For nitrogen? Or potassium? I would have thought the soil would be chockablock."

I shook my head. "Not in the area I'm planting. The soil's been leached of nutrients, like you'd see in a rainforest. I think it's a microclimate thing—maybe that area receives more irrigation." The hothouse ceiling was rigged with a watering system, so that the whole room got a brief spell of rain every few hours. I'd discovered that a few days ago, when I'd taken Midge for her morning walk wearing a floaty tea dress and come back dressed like a wet rat. Ever since then I'd made sure to bring an umbrella with me on our walks.

"Huh." Joanna's swirls pulsed greeny-gold as she thought that over. "Yes, I suppose that could happen. And you just so happened to pick that spot." My insides slowed, went cold. Did she doubt me?

I shrugged. "Just my luck."

"Fascinating." She sounded her usual, chipper self—didn't she?

"Yup."

"Anything else?" she asked. "All the other tests seemed normal?"

I still couldn't read her. I could feel my face heating, and I willed myself to relax. "Normal enough. Maybe a tiny bit low on magnesium? Could I get Epsom salts for that? And sulfur, to lower the pH." No need for the Epsom salts; it was just to throw her off.

She turned reddish gold: Joanna in working mode. "Sure—one order of nitrate of potash and Epsom salts coming up, with a side of sulfur."

All signs pointed to her believing me. Still, it took a few long minutes before my pulse finally slowed. I was playing with fire, in more ways than one.

Two semesters back, I'd taken a course in ecological agriculture with a man named Professor Thoner. It was in that class that I'd learned the basics of soil chemistry and plant pathology—all interesting stuff, don't get me wrong, but the real reason anyone was in the class was that Thoner was infamous on campus for being an explosives-obsessive.

That had always struck me as a funny sort of combination: someone who both enjoyed nurturing plants and blowing things up. Thoner himself had told us there was clearly some inclination towards explosives in his bloodline, as foretold by his surname, which supposedly descended from the word for *thunder* in Old English. "And there has always been this linguistic linking between the concepts of thunder and detonation," he'd narrated on a tangent to our goggle-eyed class. "*Tonare* in Latin is *to thunder*, for instance. Then you look naturally to *detonare*, which means *to thunder forth*—or, put more plainly, *to detonate*. You see?"

That seemed like more than a bit of a stretch to me, but perhaps there was something there. What was undeniable was the connection between fertilizers and explosives. Ammonium nitrate, Thoner told us cheerfully one day in the greenhouse, was not only an excellent fertilizer, but also enjoyed a secondary form of popularity among militant terrorists. Timothy McVeigh had bought two thousand pounds of the stuff for use in the Oklahoma City bombing back in the nineties, and a man in Norway had used three times that amount in a 2011 bombing, as well as six thousand pounds of ammonium nitrate's cousin, calcium ammonium nitrate—another fertilizer. Thoner liked to throw out these factoids during class for use later as extra-credit questions, so we all made sure to scribble them down dutifully alongside our notes on weed management and crop rotation.

In fact, Thoner informed us, any number of the items we might use to make explosives could also be used to coax plants to good health. Cream of tartar repelled ants. Flowers of sulfur prevented crop-killing molds. Hydrogen peroxide could be used as a foliar spray. Gypsum aided seed emergence. In stunned fascination, we all listened to his anecdotes of mixing this substance with that. As for Thoner's own credentials as an amateur bomb maker, half the class thought he was all talk, and the other half was sure he had a makeshift lab somewhere stuffed to the gills with homebrewed TNT and dynamite. Typical rumors about professors tend towards the titillating variety—a blow job for a grade boost, that sort of thing. The rumor about Thoner was that a couple years ago he'd invited a select group of students to his house out in the middle of nowhere—not for blow jobs, but rather to blow things up. Montana has a lot of land in private possession; it was plausible enough. Whatever the real truth, everyone was in agreement that Thoner was on some government watch list—likely several.

So this was how I'd come to have memorized the simple recipe for gunpowder. In the proper ratios, nitrate of potash (also known as saltpeter) combined with sulfur and charcoal to make humanity's simplest low-level explosive. The saltpeter supplied the oxygen, and the sulfur and charcoal burned.

I didn't want to cause the *Huivnarrut* to explode—really, truly I didn't. I'd considered ammonium nitrate for a moment, but it was too notorious, too powerful. Joanna might grow suspicious, and if she did supply it to me I'd blow myself to smithereens trying to escape. But I did desperately need a tool on hand to help get me off this ship before we left Earth for good.

Gunpowder was only half of the equation, though. I needed something to burn or blast to aid in my escape. Until last night, I hadn't known what that something was.

But now I knew of that sad room below, the room that had been rended into ugly, mismatched pieces by—that part of the puzzle I didn't know yet. But what I did know was the cold that filled that room, the air sweet and icy and fresh despite the hum of the engines underfoot. A familiar kind of cold.

My cold.

And I was willing to bet—would *have* to bet—that it wouldn't take much to break through to the other side.

Chapter Twenty

I had a free half hour before Del and I had agreed to meet. Apparently we were to use the sim room again, which meant another swimsuit to allow the nanobots enough skin contact to work their magic. I kept up an absentminded conversation with Joanna while she whipped up an outfit for me—this time a deep burgundy one-piece with numerous straps and mesh cut-outs. There were many thoughts in my mind all clamoring for attention: gunpowder, kayaking… and, for a surprising moment, the look in Del's eyes when he'd asked me if I'd like to use the sim room again.

"You seem distracted," said Joanna as the fabricator dinged.

"Wondering what Del has planned." He'd said it would be "fearsome," if memory served correctly.

"Oh, don't worry about that!" she chortled. "It's just a simulation—can't harm you." But it could scare me. "Try on the suit."

It took me longer than I'd like to admit to figure out how to put this new swimsuit on; no matter which hole I put my arms and head through, there always seemed to be a strap hanging loose. Finally I had an epiphany that the last strap was supposed to go cross-body, over my head, and I was in. Let no man say that fashion is for the brainless.

I took a look at myself in the magic mirror. "No one would wear this to go swimming. This is just lingerie." Lingerie that was doing wonders for my cleavage, and I didn't even have the filters turned up.

"That," said Joanna haughtily, "is an Alexander McQueen swimwear original, designed as an exclusive gift for Alessandra Ambrosio. It is not 'just lingerie.'" I considered that Joanna might be getting too big for her virtual britches.

"If I wore this to the beach I'd get arrested for public indecency."

"It is *Alexander McQueen*," she repeated as if that meant something to me, which it did not. High fashion in my neck of the woods meant Target instead of Walmart.

Good ol' Alexander, was what I wanted to say, but I contained myself to spare her feelings. "Right." Then I obediently slipped on the new cover-up to match, this one just as flimsy as the last.

"It's perfect," sighed Joanna, pink tendrils wiggling.

I pulled the cover-up close around me. "It's cold is what it is."

"Don't worry about that; you'll heat up in no time, what the master has you doing." What was that supposed to mean? "Ah, here he comes now."

True to her word, Del strode through my door a moment later, clad in his shorter sim-room trousers. I had a briefly terrifying moment where I wondered if he had any suspicion of our nine—nine!—minutes alone together last night, but his face betrayed no memory. He did stop almost mid-stride, though, to take in my outfit, the fur around his face and atop his shoulders puffing. "This attire..." he started. In my peripheral vision, I could see the pink of Joanna's geometries flushing a dark fuchsia.

"It's Alexander McQueen," I said airily with a flap of my hand.

"It is a handsome look."

"Thank you."

"But also a bold look. This Alexander McQueen seems a visionary. It is something a female rumae might don, were she human."

"I'm dressed by the best in interstellar fashion," I said and motioned to the wall where Joanna wriggled pinkly, soaking up her praises.

He shot her a look. "I see that. Are you ready?"

"Ready as ever."

Back down to the lowest floor we went. I knew the drill now—off with the cover-up, on with the goggles and the gold dust. Once we were properly gilded, I turned to Del. The gold flecks on his body highlighted the powerful cords of muscle beneath his skin. In a different setting he'd be a movie star, being airbrushed with body makeup by a dutiful, underpaid intern.

Cut that out. Focus. "So what's this fearsome activity?" I asked rather forcefully as I dragged my eyes back upwards—only to find that his focused gaze also made me want to squirm. Lord, what was going on?

"Why are you looking at me like that?" he asked.

"Like what?"

"You're not blinking. You look pained. It is... odd."

"*You're* odd." Oh good, middle school insults. "I'm fine.

What's… what's the fearsome activity?"

"I don't think you will like it." So he said; the look in his eyes dared me to do otherwise. "You wouldn't rather go down the other fork in the river?"

"Try me."

With a quiet command in Ziryahshun the walls of the sim room became dense jungle, the ceiling above us transforming into a twisted canopy of trees that allowed dappled glimpses of a milky, purple-gray sky. I'd viewed Tenctah from space; now I saw it from ground level. The air around us was heavy with humidity, the smell an entire life cycle of plants sprouting, living, and decaying. And all around me the sounds of uncountable, unknown beasts twined together into a natural symphony: screeches, belches, chirps, grumbles, sighs, croaks.

The light in the jungle was dim, but I could still see reasonably well, aided by the luminescent vines and growths I'd come to know from the ship's hothouse. They lit up the deeper pockets of foliage like night-lights. I gasped as a glowing bluey-green streak flowed toward us from the left; it was a swarm of floating, betentacled creatures, each as large and plump as a clementine. They darted around us curiously like a school of fish; one or two brushed my cheek with velvet-soft tentacles before the whole group of them darted away.

"What are they?" I whispered, awestruck.

"They are called *hunar im*," he said in a low tone, "or simply im. They are a great aid in pollination, I think somewhat similar to Earth's…" He tilted his head, waiting for his translation tech to supply the answer, but I beat him to it.

"They're like bees." He made a quick motion for me to lower my voice. I glanced around us; what else lurked nearby, maybe listening for a tasty snack?

"Yes," he said softly, "bees. The brushing of the ims' tentacles from one plant to the next allows the pollination to occur." My head swam; it was all so familiar yet so foreign. Sister planets—that was more and more what Earth and Tenctah seemed to me to be.

"So what are we doing here?" I asked, looking him over. The simulation had dressed Del in dark, loose pants, a matching top, and sturdy boots; he looked rather like a bulky tai-chi master about to go hiking. Glancing down, I saw that my outfit matched his. I rubbed the material between my fingers; it was thin as silk but oddly robust-feeling. A strange bit of metal on a long cord hung around my neck; Del wore one just like it.

And at our feet sat a large black chest, which Del opened to reveal…

I sucked in a breath. *Weapons*. Knives glittered and guns gleamed, many outfitted with high-tech gauges and bright displays.

"I surrender," I said, taking a step backward. I still had strong memories of trying to shoot Del that first time I'd seen him, and I remembered just as strongly the ease with which he'd divested me of my gun. Anyone who bet on me to win in a duel against Del would have had to be dropped on their head at birth.

"We're on the same team," he said in a murmur, laughter lining his words. "We're here to fight—" And here he said a few syllables that I didn't catch.

"Come again?"

"*Uriku val*," he said again, slower this time. "Canopy-dwelling val."

"Oh my," I said, wide-eyed. "I've always heard the canopy-dwelling val are much fiercer than the cliff-dwelling val."

"That is… true," he said, giving me a disbelieving look. "How did you—? Ah, it is a joke."

"That's right," I said dryly. "So we're going to kill these val for sport?"

"Yes. Were they real, we would feast on their hearts afterwards."

"Of course." I was sure this must be Tenctah humor, but he didn't blink. "Oh! Oh." Ew. "Do you cook the hearts first?"

"Cooking the hearts is a necessity. The raw flesh and organs of the val contain a poison that's neutralized in the cooking process."

"Well, thank goodness for that." Del nodded in stern agreement as I fought competing desires to laugh or cry. Then he turned to the weapons chest and began assessing its contents, all while telling me about our enemy *du jour*.

Val were a winged species with beaky heads, thick necks, long claws, and barbed tails—these claws and tails perfectly formed for lashing their enemies' flesh into ribbons. Their grayish flesh was thick and rubbery, he told me, though there was a weak spot on the underbelly with thinner skin. Canopy-dwelling val were a smaller variety than their cliff-dwelling brethren, to allow for easier maneuvering through the thick jungle, but their wingspan could still reach upwards of five feet across. Weak eyesight and little-to-no sense of smell weren't impediments to the val, as their keen hearing allowed them to form highly accurate auditory maps of their surroundings. This was the reason to keep our voices down; if the val suspected we were in the area, they might leave for other parts.

"But we will also use their hearing to our advantage," he said. "These whistles"—ah, so that's what our pendants were for—"closely approximate the sound of a young val in distress. And as the val are highly protective of their young—"

"They're going to be dive-bombing us to save fake val babies."

"Correct."

"Good thing we're wearing armor," I said, motioning at our thin tai-chi garb. I supposed that was a macho part of the challenge—to not only make the val hopping mad, but to face their mama-bear furor wearing wholly inappropriate clothing.

"That's right," Del nodded, all serious, then he did a little double-take. Earth humor strikes again. "Oh, you mean… The material stiffens and hardens in response to objects that might pierce the flesh."

"Objects that might pierce the flesh," I repeated stupidly. He found this sort of thing fun?

"Yes, such as the val's tail and talons." His brow furrowed. "Weren't you listening? The val—"

"No, I heard you," I said with a wave of my hand. "Just taking it all in. So you blow the whistle, the val go apeshit, and we kill them."

"Yes. *Ape-shit*," he said slowly, feeling out the syllables. "An interesting word. They will be incensed and attack, and then we will kill them. As for how *you* will kill them…" He reached into the weapons chest and brought out a techy-looking blunderbuss, with a flared muzzle and an array of red lights down its length. "This will suit you well. Not too large, easy to use, easy to aim." I took it from him carefully. The "not too large" gun was still large enough that I needed both hands to hold it steady. Gripping it felt strange, much less comfortable than any of Dad's rifles, and I realized with a chill that this was a weapon that had been shaped and weighted for beings not human.

"Try holding it like this," Del said, seeing me adjust my grip this way and that. He reached out and nudged my right hand back a bit. My left hand he moved forward to cover a few of the shaft's glowing lights.

Next he tapped the forefinger of my left hand. "Push in." I did so and felt the warm light under my fingertip click inward: a button. "That sets the gun on its the lowest power," he said. "An attack to stun and incapacitate. Try the next setting." I clicked in my middle finger. "That's one level up, meant to heavily wound or kill. It will have a low amount of spread. Use it for a single enemy. The next finger, then…" I clicked it in. "This attack will have a wider spread, to annihilate multiple enemies. It is dangerous to use alongside a brother-in-arms, due to the risk of friendly fire. Best for you to stay at the first setting, I think."

Fine by me. Next he tapped a little switch on top, and a square plane of light a few inches across sprang into view over the gun, displaying an illuminated version of the dark jungle before us.

"I'll look through this when aiming?" I guessed, holding the gun aloft to peer through the light scope.

"Yes," he said, his gaze on me assessing. "But…" And then with a quick step he came around behind me, his arms enfolding me as if to hug me from behind. The solidity of his chest bumped against my back, his arms on either side of me thick and strong. His hands curled around my own—warm!—adjusting my hold on the weapon once more: up this way, around that way. "There," he said softly after a moment. He was so close that his words rumbled through me. "You must…" His breath seemed to catch; he gave a slight cough. "You must remember to hold it this way. The angle must both allow a natural aim as well as easy sight through the scope. And this here," he said, tapping the trigger where my index finger rested, "will fire." Then he stepped away from me. There and gone again—the sudden negative space of the warm jungle air at my back was somehow just as shocking.

"Okay," I said shakily, trying to memorize the grip, trying to remember that we were about to purposefully enrage some monstrous flying beasts, even as all my thoughts tumbled down one long hole to a place shadowed and untraveled: Del's hands nudging mine into place around the gun, the way he'd started his sentence, caught himself up, begun again. Simple things, little things—each one as inconsequential and light as a pebble, but pooled together sat with me, heavily.

"Now point the gun at me," he said.

I blinked. "Sounds like a bad idea."

"Point it," he ordered, and I reluctantly swung my aim towards him. Del lit up like white flame on the scope.

"Oh!"

"They will look just like that," he said, to my relief side-stepping away from my gun, "but red."

"So shoot the red?"

"Shoot the red."

"I can do that."

"We will see if you can," he said, eyeing me with interest. Then he grabbed some wicked-looking, barbed brass knuckles from the weapons chest, blew his whistle, and our hunt began.

Whenever my parents had taken me to Chuck E. Cheese as a kid, I'd always loved the *Jurassic Park* game best, which ate tokens like candy. In the game, you faced down a proto-VR slew of velociraptors, triceratops, and T-rexes with a plastic laser gun. I remembered my mom taking control of one gun and me taking the other. Copious amounts of vibrant purple dinosaur blood spattered the camera as we gunned down half the park.

That's how I tried to calm myself as Del brought the whistle to his lips and blew. This was just an advanced version of that janky Chuck E. Cheese game: Step One, see an alien pterodactyl; Step Two, shoot the alien pterodactyl.

The whistle made an odd, high, bleating noise, and the whole jungle held its breath around us. Then from the high reaches of the canopy came a distant, layered crooning.

Del made a quick motion toward my whistle: *you try*. Hesitantly, I lifted the whistle to my lips and blew another thin note. *Again*, he signaled to me, and, wincing, I obliged. The crooning above us deepened, intensified—approached. I flinched when the sparse light filtering through the leaves to light our little clearing was briefly severed by a quick, shadowed movement from above.

A quiet moment. Another.

Del raised his whistle once more…

And then the first val plunged down into our clearing, croaking an adult version of our fake whistle calls. The val was smaller than the nightmarish vision Del's description had painted, but not by much. It was an ugly thing, its hairless skin a concrete gray marred with bruise-colored splotches down the spine. Black, beady, useless-looking eyes were set on each side of its weighty head. It flapped about our clearing like a bat out of hell, caroming off trees, its heavy, heaving wing coming within millimeters of slapping me across the face. A spray of wood splinters flew through the air; its tail had gouged the branch to my left.

With a jolt I remembered to lift the gun, and the val's body lit up fluorescent red in the scope, a decided improvement on its ugliness. Step One, then Step Two: my finger tightened on the trigger, and a rushing blast exploded from the gun. It had been a good hit, I thought, but the shot seemed to do little more than daze the val momentarily. It shook its head and gave an all-body shiver of rage; I saw the quick tensing of muscles coiling to attack…

Yet a moment was all Del needed. He leapt towards the val with both arms outstretched, and then the two of them became a thrashing blur. He was pummeling the val about the head, the deadly combination of his claws and the brass knuckles sending bluish droplets flying: blue, I noticed in my horror-induced stupor, not purple. The val whipped about in Del's grasp as it tried to free itself, and its tail caught at my leg, sending me crashing to the forest floor. It was a hit meant to leave anything in its wake a mangled mess, but my frantic fumbling at my leg to check for damage revealed unmarred skin: the miracle of the fabric we wore.

The val gave a piercing shriek, and from the corner of my eye I saw more blue blood spray through the air, coating a tree across the clearing like someone had decided to give it a paint job.

Well, let Del have at it; he seemed to have the situation well in hand. There was a tree at my back; I sank against it and moaned when my clothes hardened uncomfortably in response to the gravelly prick of the bark, like I was being repelled from the tree. The universe was conspiring to keep me participating in this awfulness, it seemed. I gritted my teeth and rose to my feet again.

The val had found a second wind and freed itself from Del's grasp. Now it was flapping around just above his head, trying to rake him with its talons. I took a shot at the val and missed, took another shot that did not. The val sank like a stone…

Del was on it in a flash. A roar—a high, terrible scream… I turned my head just in time as there came one last thumping blow, accompanied by a percussive, bone-crushing finality.

Our clearing was blessed by a momentary silence—then a few more val plummeted down to avenge their fallen compatriot, and our clearing became a seething mass of gray wings.

The only nice thing that could really be said about the val was that they were so awful that I felt no compunction about killing them. Like a hydra with its infinite heads, we always seemed to take care of one val only for two more to show up. Amidst the onslaught, Del and I fell into a horrid little "I stun them, you kill them" routine. The gun's scope became my best friend; with the val in red relief against the backdrop of the jungle, I found that I wasn't a half-bad shot. And Del was always there in the fray, lit up in glowing white. Watching him fight was a sight to behold, and it became obvious why he enjoyed hunting the val: he was just so good at it. Sure, I was "helping," but he would have been fine without me.

That's what I thought until two of the val got smart and teamed up for a coordinated attack. One was a great, hulking sucker bigger than the others; it performed a snarling, spitting display across the clearing to grab Del's attention while its slighter friend crept up slowly along the forest floor, wings flattened back to keep a low profile. My angle was terrible; shooting at the sneaking val would just as likely end up hitting Del. And I could see he was unaware of the second val behind him, unaware of how its wicked tail twitched eagerly, preparing to attack.

In that moment my mind became a big, smooth blank: no thoughts, no words. I was leaping forward, I was straddling the val's back, I was pinning it to the ground as it writhed beneath me, flipped around, shrieked and shrieked and shrieked. Talons were trying to tear through my shirt into my stomach—

And then it was gone, ripped away from me by Del. He grasped the val's tail with both hands—never mind the barbs—and whipped its body against a tree trunk one, two, three times before dropping the whole thing to the ground.

There was another crystalline silence that I was certain would shatter into more carnage. This one held, though; no more val dared invade our clearing. From behind me I could hear the softest *drip... drip... drip...* I didn't have to turn my head to know that it was the other val, the one that had distracted Del, its blood now making a dark mud of the forest floor.

"They're all dead," he said unnecessarily. He stood a few yards from me, blue blood smeared on him like war paint.

"Yeah." That was the best he was going to get; my body was humming in anticipation of the next attack, every nerve feeling like it was about to spit sparks. My brain buzzed as if it were filled with angry bees.

He moved closer and took the gun from me. I made a faint noise of protest; that was my weapon. I needed it. "They're all dead," he repeated, tossing the gun to the ground, along with his brass knuckles. "You— That last..."

He eyed the spot where I'd wrestled with the val. The ground, once virgin, was now a churned mess of moss and upturned dirt.

"Why didn't you shoot it?" he asked, looking back to me again.

I shook my head at his astonished expression. Was this not obvious? "You were too close."

His rumbling growl sent a wave of shivers tumbling over me. Just like I'd come to read Joanna, to know her moods and feelings at a glance, so too had the beastly, alien planes of Del's face become familiar to me, and he looked at me now with indescribable frustration.

"The gun distinguishes friend from foe on its lower two power levels," he said. His voice was tight, like he was straining to keep from shouting. "If you see an enemy, you shoot it. The gun will take care of the rest. There is no need for—for valiant tussling in the dirt."

Oh. "Oh," I said, wilting, before I remembered that, hang on now, he hadn't *told* me any of this. My lessons in alien weaponry had lasted all of a minute, give or take. "Well, you didn't say that!" I said, tipping my chin up to treat him to a fiery stare of my own.

"But I did," he said. His pupils had gone wide, nearly eclipsing the vermilion band around them.

I consulted my memory and was disappointed to discover that he wasn't wrong, on the barest technicality. In my book, saying that the highest power level on the gun had the potential for friendly fire wasn't exactly the same as saying the gun's other settings *didn't* have that potential. I narrowed my eyes.

"But you didn't say that, not really. And it worked out all right in the end, so what do you care? The val's dead, right? Plus it's *just a simulation*—isn't that what you're always saying? So how about you stop yelling at me, and—"

"My lovely, irascible human," he interrupted, and I just

about rolled my eyes at *irascible*—such a Del word—before my brain realized I'd skipped headlong over that first adjective. "You are going to be the death of me," he finished.

And then he bent his great head downward, and his lips found mine.

His kiss began slowly: a grazing of warmth against my lips, the soft lick of his tongue against the seam of my mouth, a gentle, silent question…

I opened to him. He tasted like… It was like something I'd always sought without realizing it, a misty longing explored in dreams and then forgotten. He tasted wild, fiercely male… desirous. And something dormant within me was unfolding, unfurling, billowing outward with a burning ferocity. It filled me up, lit my skin aflame, pushed me into him. One taste would never be enough—I needed to know him in a way that one kiss would never satisfy, and needed him to know me, too.

What had started soft became urgent. I'd been kissed before, of course, and had never loved tongue—had always felt it was the sort of thing I was supposed to do, rather than really wanted to do—but his was making me quake. And then I slowed, remembering that—that— Very carefully, I felt along the edge of his teeth with my tongue, shivering when I reached a sharp fang. He stilled for a moment, then caught at my lip, playing, and I moaned. I felt his low laugh more than I heard it, and he teased me slowly once more, feeling the fullness of my lip, before moving into me again. His hands were running over me, pulling me to the hard muscle of his body, then moving upward to feel the fine silk of my hair… Which made me remember something else, and I reached up to him, exploring the shaggy tangle of his mane.

And a heavy, hot thrum was building inside me, and I wondered… I wondered…

Then there came a muted, hesitant dinging, like an abashed summoning bell, and he jerked away from me, breathing hard. I stumbled a bit, trying to find my feet; I was jelly-legged. Sometime in the midst of it all, the blood-soaked jungle had melted away into nothingness, leaving us back in the plain sim room—whose normally white corners, I saw in my peripheral vision, quivered with the most delicate mix of pink and sherbet orange. Oh, good Lord. I reached for my discarded cover-up in the corner of the room and wrapped it around me tightly, wishing it were opaque, wishing I weren't aching at the abrupt end of—whatever had just happened.

Del gave a word of assent, and the walls lit up with brighter, twisting orange. "Apologies, master, Corinne," Joanna said. Her next sentence was in rapid Ziryahshun, not a word of which I recognized. Del's fuming response, though, was easy enough to understand; apparently, *ghar* meant "fuck." I liked that; the similarity to "grrr" seemed appropriate.

They went back and forth for a minute, Del pacing the edges of the small room while I stood in the middle, waiting to be enlightened. Did this seeming catastrophe have anything to do with me? It was infuriating to be in the dark.

At last the walls went a deeper red—ominous—and Del

ceased his pacing. "What's happening?" I asked.

He glared silently into the corner of the room.

"What's happening?" I repeated, dipping my head into his line of vision. Now he was glaring at me. "Whatever it is, it can't be *that* bad." Could it?

"My mother grows anxious for my return to Ailopt," he said slowly.

The air in the room seemed to go suddenly thin. "Oh? Are we… leaving now?"

"No! No," he said with a start, obviously realizing how that must have sounded. My heart slowed a pace. "Don't worry. We're staying here, on Earth. But my mother… she has sent someone to spy on me, to observe the status quo, and I've just had to grant permission to board." His frown deepened as his gaze wandered over me—my flimsy clothing, my mussed hair. "You should go to your suite. And stay there."

I bristled. "Surely that's not necessary. You're the vra-khinahar! Don't you outrank this spy? Can't you just tell them to, you know… fuck off?"

A muscle twitched under his eye when Joanna cut in again. "She's boarding. She's also brought a drone…" she said in a light tone.

She? "Del, who is this spy?" I asked lightly, as I envisioned a female rumae in a dominatrix costume stalking down the *Huivnarrut*'s halls (don't ask me where I get these thoughts), relaying her report to the central intelligence office through an earpiece.

He scowled. "There is no helping it. You need to head back

upstairs. She's a terrible busybody. Scheming. The worst of them all."

Strange way to put it. "The worst of *who* all? *Who is it?*"

His expression turned tortured. "Jexrah. My sister."

Thank you so much for reading *Unearthly*! If you enjoyed this book and have a spare moment, I'd love it if you would write a review on Goodreads or wherever you bought the book. Reviews are key to helping new readers discover my books. Also, if you want to be notified about new releases, sign up for my newsletter at katiejgallagher.com or follow me on Amazon or Facebook!

Also, for a **free ebook copy** of *Starcrossed*, the second book in the Beauty and Her Alien series, head to **KatieJGallagher.com/free**. Happy reading!

And again, thank you so much for spending time with my book! That means the entire world to me.

All the best,
Katie

Acknowledgments

I am incredibly grateful to everyone around me who has supported me in making this series a reality. Writing books is like running a marathon, and it would never be possible without the amazing people in my life.

An enormous, wholehearted thank you to my readers for your enthusiasm and support. It is incredible to know that there are people all around the world reading and enjoying my books. More to come!

Many thanks to Tanya Chris, for being my bestest writing buddy along the way, and to Sammy, for providing us his invaluable feline assistance whenever we've written together these past years.

Thank you also to my NaNo CT North crew: Marina Black, Chelsea, Auny, Kat, and everybody else.

Thanks also to Joanna Penn, for giving her blessing for Joanna to remain the character that she is. Yes, perhaps Joanna will take over the world—only time will tell!

Serious thanks to LianaM at 99designs for her incredible cover designs. The work you do is magical—no other word for it.

Thank you to all the writers out there who have crafted iterations of this tale. There are many, *many* versions of Beauty and the Beast, and I read as many retellings as I could get my hands on during the drafting of this series for inspiration.

Thanks and remembrance to Rhapsody, who served as inspiration for Midge and passed during the writing of this series. You are so missed.

To my parents, sister, grandparents, and everyone else in my family, many, many thanks. A shoutout especially to my mom for serving as my gardening expert and fielding all my weird plant questions. I am not a gardener, and somehow I have crafted a story that revolves heavily around plants (huge facepalm).

And, most importantly, thank you to my husband, John. Were it not for your excellent and unflinching advice, Corinne's story would be half of what it is today.

KATIE JANE GALLAGHER is the author of BBNYA finalist *Specter*, the *Beauty and Her Alien* series, and *The Gold in the Dark*. She was born and raised in Illinois, and the magical Naperville Public Library was her home away from home until she ventured to the East Coast for college. Katie graduated magna cum laude from Connecticut College with a BA in Chinese language and literature. She currently lives in Connecticut with her stupendous, half-human half-neanderthal husband and their dopey boxer dog.

You can sign up for Katie's newsletter and get
a **free ebook copy of *Starcrossed***, the next
book in the *Beauty and Her Alien* series, here:

KATIEJGALLAGHER.COM/FREE

www.ingramcontent.com/pod-product-compliance
Lightning Source LLC
Chambersburg PA
CBHW021128190726
48288CB00008B/2558